M000187292

Victoria Kreysar is an established scholar and educator. She holds degrees in history and secondary education, graduating with distinction from Mercyhurst University. A former international art dealer, Ms. Kreysar is a noted adventurer and explorer, having worked as a ship hand aboard tall ships and lived for extended periods in Greece, Montenegro, Italy, Spain, Croatia, France, and the Caribbean. When not writing, she spends her time swimming, scuba diving, and enjoying a good book.

To my family, Courtney John, and Winnie

Victoria Kreysar

GENESIS

AUSTIN MACAULEY PUBLISHERS™

LONDON · CAMBRIDGE · NEW YORK · SHARJAH

Copyright © Victoria Kreysar (2021)

All rights reserved. No part of this publication may be reproduced, distributed, or transmitted in any form or by any means, including photocopying, recording, or other electronic or mechanical methods, without the prior written permission of the publisher, except in the case of brief quotations embodied in critical reviews and certain other noncommercial uses permitted by copyright law. For permission requests, write to the publisher.

Any person who commits any unauthorized act in relation to this publication may be liable to criminal prosecution and civil claims for damages.

This is a work of fiction. Names, characters, businesses, places, events, locales, and incidents are either the products of the author's imagination or used in a fictitious manner. Any resemblance to actual persons, living or dead, or actual events is purely coincidental.

Ordering Information
Quantity sales: Special discounts are available on quantity purchases by corporations, associations, and others. For details, contact the publisher at the address below.

Publisher's Cataloging-in-Publication data
Kreysar, Victoria
Genesis

ISBN 9781647502744 (Paperback)
ISBN 9781647502737 (Hardback)
ISBN 9781647502751 (ePub e-book)

Library of Congress Control Number: 2020925022

www.austinmacauley.com/us

First Published (2021)
Austin Macauley Publishers LLC
40 Wall Street, 33rd Floor, Suite 3302
New York, NY 10005
USA

mail-usa@austinmacauley.com
+1 (646) 5125767

Christopher

Chapter One

The professor sat in his office, staring at his computer, not looking at the screen but slightly above it. Pictures, cards, mementos of all kinds hung around him, testaments to accomplishments and relationships that had piled up through the years. Teaching awards and family photos, history jokes given to him by students, class schedules and rubrics, department notices that seemed important at the time, even university letters that were too comical to be legitimate hung from tacks on the corkboards. One small letter sat in the corner just above his computer, lost among the colors of keepsakes deemed worthy to make the cut of the corkboard of memories. Inside, the letter was a handwritten note, and it held the gaze of the professor, scribbled in perfect cursive letters, signed with a six-letter first name and nothing more. His eyes drifted over it often, especially these past few weeks.

He was a sturdy man, standing several inches over six feet, still managing to stand straight and walk without too much trouble, although his bad knee sometimes reminded him of his age. He was not old by any means, but he certainly was not young. The years had been kind to him, only his eyesight and hairline had felt the burden of time. It was more stubbornness than pride which caused him to rarely wear his glasses and shave his hair; simple solutions to somewhat complex problems. He had dark-brown eyes that looked black depending on the lighting, but they lit up when he spoke of things he loved, which he often did. With a deep voice and his somewhat-imposing form, students often hesitated before entering his office or approaching him after a lecture.

The distant thunder outside warned of a summer storm approaching. The professor didn't mind though; he was safe and dry in his office which smelled of paper, ink, and the tangerines he had a habit of snacking on. The books stacked in floor-to-ceiling bookshelves along the wall opposite to the desk begged to be read, but his eyes knew better than to think they could. One book in particular sat on the top shelf, bound in leather, its pages threatening to bust out of their binding with their contents: secrets, old and new and forbidden. The professor knew he should never write them down, but somewhere in his hasty youthful pursuit, he found himself caught up in research and couldn't resist the urge to commit the words to paper.

It was all secretive of course, one mystery leading to another, and a lie sprinkled in here and there, not even his research assistant knew the real reasoning behind it. The university had given him money, and who was he to refuse the gift of a research grant?

Being a history professor wasn't exciting outside of the normal realm of academia. But this, what the professor had in his head, threatened to topple that. Very rarely do ancient texts and ledgers result in a paper that not only gets published but read worldwide. Historians have a slim audience unless they stumble onto something almost magical.

No one would read the journal, no one would even find it or know what they had found. No one but her and perhaps a few others. He made the decision several weeks ago to go public with his knowledge; he figured since it was his own decision, he had control over it still. He could choose what to reveal and what to conceal. Enough to make headlines and attract some attention, but hopefully not too much. He knew the challenge he faced; he was a historian after all, with all that contained, but nothing more.

Numerous papers had been published over the years, all bearing his name and sometimes other colleagues. It was only once he made the mistake of letting their names go before his in a book; after the larger portion of work went to him along with the smallest cut of the royalties, he preferred to work alone. It started out small enough, this project. It was innocent, as most things are. It was a long time ago, but, to historians, time doesn't matter as much as people think it does.

Five interviews; that was all he was giving. He knew, by the fifth interview, the world would be watching. How could they not be? Only two interviews had been done, and already the world was beginning to buzz, to hum with words and thoughts over his findings.

A news story blared from the screen of the professor's computer, but, still, his eyes could focus on nothing except the small note on his corkboard.

Sharp knocking on his door jolted him out of his thoughts, finally removing his eyes from the note. He glanced at the clock sitting next to his tired coffeemaker with spilt sugar still crusted beside it.

Yes, it was time for the third interview. The leather chair squeaked in protest as he stood. Before opening the door, he straightened his black dress shirt and glanced down at his gray dress pants, making sure they looked presentable. He was not a vain man, but he liked to look nice. He knew his age walked the fine line between women looking at him and women overlooking him. The gold wedding ring sat uncomfortably on his finger, not used to being worn, although he'd had the same one for over 30 years now, making sure to wear it when necessary.

Today, it was necessary for him to put his best foot forward. The world had to know what he knew, or at least what he was willing to tell.

Chapter Two

Harlow knew she should have tied her shoelaces tighter, but she didn't have time to worry about her black Chuck Taylor flopping with her feet as she raced down the alleyway. The green numbers from the digital watch on her wrist read 11:39 as they poked out from underneath the black sweatshirt that hugged her slim frame.

Six minutes. She had to stay out of their reach for six more minutes.

The alarm from the jewelry store blared, and she thought the entire portion of the city would be awoken. Damn, that would really mess up her plans. No one ever takes into account the volume of the alarms when planning a robbery, but she made a mental note to add it to her scouting next time. And, she promised herself, there would be a next time.

Harlow was dressed entirely in black, unable to resist the cliché of a thief wearing black; she did, however, manage to refrain from adding the ski mask. She had tried it once but quickly discovered the nighttime was all she needed to hide with. That and a good plan.

Her dark-brown eyes took in the surroundings, her feet never lessening their pace. She knew it was just the adrenaline keeping her going; running was never her forte.

Recognizing the darkest street was to her right, she quickly turned and ran down it, eager to avoid the police and their noisy cars as they tried to catch up to her.

A stack of newspapers sat piled up in front of a small bodega, still open at this hour, but the street was deserted. Without a single sound except the thump of her loose sneaker, Harlow leapt from one stack to the next, jumping with all her might, smiling as she felt her hands connect to the low-hanging fire escape. The heavy book bag protested that gravity was in fact against this plan, but Harlow forced her legs to swing up and over a metal bar until she, and the book bag, were firmly seated on the metal grating. Pulling her hood tighter around her face, she curled up, safely hidden from view.

She checked her watch; only four more minutes. Taking deep breaths to calm herself, she leaned back, feeling the hard cargo still securely locked away inside her backpack. It was, after all, what had gotten her into this mess in the first place.

The door to the bodega opened as the owner, or dedicated employee perhaps, stuck his head outside to see what all the commotion was. Harlow could smell the food from inside, and she realized how hungry she was; she knew heists always made her hungry, but, normally, the adrenaline staved the feeling. Praying her stomach didn't grumble too loudly in protest while silently thanking the alarm for actually being as loud as it was, she glanced down, wondering if there was perhaps a way she could steal a snack.

It was then she noticed what was smattered on the front page of the newspaper: 'The Professor Tells All.' But not just any professor, no, Harlow knew all too well the face giving the camera a half smile that hid his teeth but lit up his eyes.

Her legs screamed in protest as she swung her body backward, hooking her legs over the metal bar but lowering the rest of herself down low enough to grab a loose newspaper before launching herself back up to her hiding place.

It was him all right; she knew him well enough; the name printed below the picture meant nothing to her, but it was strange to see his full name spelled out. She'd only ever called him by that once or twice before he told her not to. They were closer than formal names, closer than a lot of people realized.

She shook the thoughts from her head. If he was talking publicly like this, she needed to talk to him too, before anyone else could. This message wasn't just for the reporters or their network consumers.

Suddenly, her watch vibrated on her arm, and the countdown of 30 seconds forced her to shove the newspaper into her backpack, next to the stolen gems, and tighten the bag back safely where it belonged. The newspaper would be worth it though, losing the gems. But she would have them both; she was a professional after all.

The watch hit zero, and Harlow heard a loud bang, then water gushing from somewhere which she knew to be a fire hydrant, then the shouts of people rushing out to see what they didn't know was wrong. It would take them days to realize the scheduled flushing of the city pipes had been hijacked by a makeshift clog that caused the entire system to backup and explode.

Harlow smiled proudly as she jumped down, no longer worried about keeping out of sight. She safely joined the growing crowd to view the commotion, watching the cops on foot run to find out what the noise had been. They would be busy for a while with this mess. She knew she could slip down the side street and away from anyone who might stop her; Harlow had a new objective, and it had nothing to do with the gems in her bag.

Chapter Three

Edward shuffled from one foot to another as he stood behind the computer at the workstation. He could feel the cement floor through the too-thin rubber mat; his back was beginning to get sore, a sure sign he needed new shoes. Or that his six-day work week needed to end soon. He could only run on five hours of sleep and two pots of coffee for so many days before his body would shut down. But today was Friday; he would have to wait until Sunday.

Sunday, he would sleep.

Finally, the clock read 1:00 which meant he was able to sneak out for lunch somewhere, and, today, anywhere was good. It was days like today he wished he still had his old life back; well, part of it at least. Edward rubbed a hand over his shaved head and readjusted the glasses he still wasn't completely used to having. Late 40s, and, now, his eyes decided they needed help. A sigh escaped his body, his shoulders rising and falling, remaining slightly curved down from the years of fighting. All the injuries he sustained, and he was lucky enough none of them were visible; even the scar above his lip from a bat to the face had faded over the years.

He decided it was time and, with a quick goodbye, left the store to ride away in his company van. It felt good to be outside in the summer heat; driving around in it with the windows down was the only bit of summer he could enjoy with his schedule, and it wouldn't be long before the snow would begin to fly.

Driving the streets of the city, eating his fast-food burger and keeping an eye on the clock, Edward couldn't help but shake the feeling of monotony seeping into his very bones. In another life, things would be different, but this was the life he had chosen. It had been different once, full of illegal activities and adrenaline rushing through his veins every day. But, now, he had a 401K and paid taxes, and retirement felt so far away.

He stopped at a red light and looked around for a spot to throw his empty wrapper, noticing some fluff news story being broadcasted from the T.V.s in the store window on the corner. An interview with a professor from the local university. His tell-all story. *What exactly would he have to tell?* Edward wondered. The life of a history professor couldn't be all that interesting.

The light turned green, but Edward didn't notice. How did he know the man was a history professor? His brain began to spin back through his memories. It was an oddly familiar sight, this man, although he was certain he'd never met him before in his life; hell, he'd dropped out of school at 16 and never bothered to go back. But, this man, he knew this man somehow. A click sounded in his brain as it froze on the memories; if Edward had hair on his head, it would have stood up, but as it was, goosebumps formed on his arms, showing outwardly how he felt internally.

Suddenly, an image of a girl with curly, brown hair, dark skin, and big eyes swam through his mind. *Her*. She bit her lip and asked too many questions and laughed with her whole body at every joke he told her.

No, Edward realized it wasn't just any professor, it was *him*, and if he was in the news, she wouldn't be too far behind. He couldn't pull his eyes from the T.V. screens, couldn't will his body to do anything but sit immobile in the shock of it all.

The car behind his silver van honked, causing his brain to snap back to the present. The light was green. His foot pushed onto the gas pedal, and he could feel his mind spin with the tires beneath him. She wasn't a part of his life anymore though, it shouldn't matter to him. She had left his life that afternoon and never come back.

Edward thought of her every day, of course, but at least he could usually push those out of his mind. He hadn't dreamt of her in a while, but, now, he was sure tonight would be different.

Chapter Four

Out on the university lawn, five boys from the baseball team were approaching a large fountain, drunkenly stumbling as they went. The tallest of the boys was leading the group, reminding them all in a not-so-silent voice that they needed to be silent lest the campus security guards overheard them and drove over to investigate. It would be difficult to explain the purpose of the XL-size dish-soap bottles that were rather obvious from their hiding places under their coats.

The tallest boy stopped for a moment as the team members continued on. It was odd, the two black SUVs parked against the curb. What could they be doing there? There we no students to be picked up from that side of campus, no parties to go to, only empty offices and classrooms at this time of night. He could faintly hear the engines running, although the headlights were off.

A yell from a more-intoxicated teammate shook the tall boy from his thoughts. He ran over to join the group, pulling out his own dish soap and shot-gunning the beer that was thrown at him.

Their voices, no longer soft, caused a moment of alarm for three people in large, black coats. They stood just inside the entrance to the supposedly empty office building. Joining them, unwillingly, was a fourth man whom the baseball boys might have recognized as the professor of U.S. History I, a class they had all failed together back during their freshman year.

"When I wished to be kidnapped, it was normally so I didn't have to come to work, yet here I am," the professor mumbled sarcastically. His only response was a grunt and a harsh jab in the ribs by a pistol. The three captors did not appreciate his dry humor.

Two men and a woman forced him roughly up the short flight of stairs and spoke in a language Dr. Tiproil couldn't understand. German, perhaps. No lights were on in the hallway, but it didn't matter; Tiproil had trod down it so many times, he could do it blindfolded. Considering this, Tiproil silently thanked his luck that he was not, in fact, blindfolded. He attempted to get a better look at who was holding him hostage.

"Turn your head or we shoot." The man who spoke had a deep, ugly scar cutting through his eyebrow. It didn't look fresh, but it couldn't be too old either.

"If you shoot me before you have what you want, how will you get it?" Another grunt was the only response to the professor's logic. "Idiots," he mumbled. If there was one thing that bothered him more than being forced against his will, it was idiocy.

The door to his office was shut and locked, like it always was when it was empty. The scarred man and the woman attempted to open the door, and both failed. The woman took a deep breath as if to calm herself before speaking.

"Open the door," she ordered. Her voice was harsh as it croaked out of her throat. The scarred man simply motioned toward the door.

"I can't." Tiproil felt the pistol dig deeper into his ribs. "When you grabbed me from the parking lot and shoved me into your smelly car, you neglected to tell me to bring my office keys."

The woman sighed. Tiproil thought, only for a moment, he saw regret flash across her face. But if he were correct, he would never have known it was regret about the sloppily laid plan, not about the kidnapping.

Another grunt. The scarred man pulled what looked almost like a cigar out of his pocket. Tiproil wondered what on earth smoking would help right now, although he couldn't deny that he could use a cigarette. The dim light that shone through the dirty windows glinted off of the cigar for a moment. Tiproil felt his stomach harden. It wasn't a cigar at all; it was a silencer for his gun.

"Shoot me, you don't get what you want," Tiproil said hastily. Suddenly, the gun pointed in his back became even more uncomfortable.

"We wanted to get in," the woman said. They were running out of time. "Do it." She nodded, and the silenced gun was fired twice, not at Tiproil, who braced himself, but at the door's lock. Metal fragments flew as the bullets smashed through. Two minutes later, the lock was no more, and the woman pushed open the door, her eagerness apparent.

They all squeezed into the office which Tiproil had repeatedly told the dean was too small. Bookcases lined the walls, leaving space for only the windows, door, and a desk.

Two empty chairs were tossed carelessly out into the hallway; they were in the way of the search.

The men and woman ransacked the office, destroying everything in their search. They never had to say what they were looking for; Tiproil knew there was only one thing they could be after. Suddenly, the scarred man brought his gloved fist through the glass-bookcase door. *Statues and Totems of the Ancient World* toppled out from the bookcase, landing face up on the carpeted floor surrounded by shards of glass that sprinkled the ground.

"You could have just opened the door," the professor said sarcastically. The pistol dug itself between his shoulder blades; another reminder not to talk.

"There's nothing here," the scarred man grunted. The woman continued to look out the window. She could just make out the outline of five boys, pouring something into the fountain.

"Check the bottom cabinet. It's locked, but you can—" There was no need for Tiproil to finish his instructions. The scarred man used the butt of his gun to smash the lock and open the door. Whatever had been inside was gone. All that remained was an empty bottle of black-label whiskey.

"Someone else has taken it," she turned around, "haven't they?"

The professor's face betrayed nothing, but a small smile spread across his thin lips.

Harlow had come. Yes, the key was gone.

"Who took it?" Her hair was a deep shade of red. Tiproil wondered if she dyed it or if it was natural; it couldn't be naturally that color, could it? Her voice was raising dangerously, but, still, Tiproil knelt silently.

He knew only part of Lo, could only ever figure out so much of her. She was selfish and unpredictable, but that's why he knew she would come to him.

"Answer me!" Her hand cracked across his face, tearing the skin around his cheek and lip.

"You won't find whatever it is you're looking for." Blood ran down, but he could not move his hands to wipe it away.

They continued to yell, destroying his office, throwing the books against the wall. He barely felt the pain in his knees from kneeling on the hard floor for so long. The voices he could tune out, but the years of work being obliterated pained him, and watching the rough, careless hands tear at his corkboard sent a stone crashing through his heart.

He closed his dark-brown eyes, unable to watch. They would not find what they were looking for. His eyes opened again when he heard the gun cock, but he did not look at the angry woman as she held her gun determinedly.

Dr. Tiproil's body had laid on the floor of his office for hours; later, when the police photographed the crime scene, they struggled to understand what they saw. The pranksters from the baseball team were long gone, their drunken memories served no assistance. Tiproil had no wedding ring on his left hand; it was still in his empty pocket. His eyes focused seemingly in the distance. Not even the detective realized they had been staring at a small note with a six-letter name signed inside.

Chapter Five

Edward snored so loud, he once had to deal with a formal noise complaint lodged from the neighbors. No matter how loud it got, he never managed to wake himself out of his slumber. Tonight, it was the unusually loud knock on the door that woke Edward from the uneasy slumber he had fallen into while collapsed on the living-room sofa. The remote had fallen from his hand onto the floor next to the dog bed which had been empty for three months now. An after-game report continued to play from the T.V., oblivious its watcher hadn't managed to stay awake for the game itself.

The knock came again, and Edward felt his brain slowly come to life. The streetlights dimly filtered through the window as Edward's eyes adjusted to the room. It was nighttime. Who could possibly be knocking at this hour? All of his friends knew he was watching the game on his own tonight.

Several empty beer bottles clanked around on the floor, caused by Edward accidentally running his foot into them on his way to the door. Cursing silently, he bent over to pick them up and stack them back against the sofa. Curiously, he heard no other noise. No beeping from his security alarm.

No more knocks. Could he have been dreaming? It was possible; he often had strange dreams, especially when he saw something that reminded him of *her*.

He sat back down and closed his eyes for a moment, wishing he was anywhere but here. Wishing his life had turned out differently. Did he want to go back to that life, a life of running and hiding and constantly worrying that someone would find him? Maybe. Maybe he missed the adrenaline. Hell, it had kept him in shape. You burn a lot of calories running from the police.

Suddenly, a loud squeak broke Edward's train of thought. Squeaking was a highly unusual sound in a home like this; outfitted with the highest and strongest security measures stolen money could afford. The squeak was coming from his kitchen. In less than 30 seconds, Edward's old instincts kicked in; the small pistol hidden in his living room was cocked.

Edward had played this moment over in his mind for years. Both he and Lo knew the goodbye they had said so long ago through tearstained faces wasn't a goodbye for good; more of a 'see you later.' Since that day, Edward's mind had concocted all sorts of scenes in which the two of them met again. Some were outdoors, surrounded by flowers and sunlight, and they kissed romantically, while others took place in a museum or even one of his shops where they simply smiled at each other for a moment before embracing. Edward's particular favorite was surprising Lo when she was out one day, catching her off guard and seeing her face light up with genuine surprise and happiness.

Out of the 79 scenarios his mind had developed, not one included him walking in on Lo breaking through the window in his kitchen on a Tuesday night after she somehow snuck through all of his security alarms.

"Holy shit," Edward's cracking voice echoed off the empty, off white walls. He noticed she still wore her Chuck Taylors, black but frayed a bit from overuse. "Holy shit." It seemed to be all he could say.

Harlow paused for a moment, one leg through the window, one outside still, her slim body resting on the ledge between. "Hi," she managed to say with a soft chuckle. Their eyes met, and Harlow smiled for a moment, feeling every emotion surge through her being; it was as if her soul was somehow screaming for his. God, had she missed him.

How long they stayed like that, neither remembered correctly. It could have been only a moment, or perhaps a lifetime. Their eyes locked on each other. Then, without warning, Harlow's Converse slipped off the edge of the sink, and her body ungracefully toppled through the window, smashing onto the tiled floor with a loud thump.

It took a moment for Edward's synapses and neurons to get his body moving again. Was it possible to go into shock from something like this? Harlow was here, on his kitchen floor, and she had not only surpassed all of his security measures and broken through the window, but she'd *left the window open*.

"Lo!" He rushed forward, clamoring over her body sprawled on the floor to yank the curtains shut. Still clutching the pistol in one hand and the blue curtains in the other, he prayed no one had seen her; but, then again, Harlow was very good at not being seen.

Slowly, he turned around, managing to string together some semblance of a sentence.

"What the hell."

"Trust me, the front door wasn't a good option," she half-whispered to the floor. One hand popped onto the countertop to hoist her body up; the other hand instantly clutching the side of her head. "You've got very solid floors."

"Tiled them myself." Edward chuckled, knowing she was all right. He knew his soul would tell him, somehow, if she was seriously hurt. They had always been connected that way. His mind continued to spin, and he forgot about the gun now sitting limply in his hand. They stood a foot apart under the dim, kitchen light. Edward was only an inch or two taller than Harlow, depending on the shoes she wore. He studied her face for some clue as to why she had shown up after all this time. Her familiar, frizzy, brown hair that she could never quite get under control was still the same it had been years before. The hand holding the gun was becoming sweaty, a symptom caused by Lo. Normally, his hands only got this sweaty when they were about to kiss.

"No." His facial expressions changed. "You need to go. Did someone see you?"

"Wha—Give me a little bit of credit, Edward. I know how to break into a home without being followed."

"The neighbors are surprisingly nosy." He nervously walked around the small kitchen, making sure every window curtain was pulled and the movement detectors still in place. "Hang on, who would have followed you?"

"What? Oh, no, I didn't mean. It's not..." she fumbled for the right phrasing. This was not going well. Her head still throbbed from where it had come into contact with the floor.

Maybe she had a concussion.

"Lo, if we are in no immediate threat from an outsider, and you didn't disable my entire security system, please just tell me what you want, so I can say no, finish drinking my beer, and go back to bed."

Lo took a breath, trying to ignore the growing pain in her head. Definitely maybe a concussion. "I need your help."

"No. No, absolutely not." He didn't move from the opposite side of the room. "Now, you can exit the way you came, through the window like a good little thief, and get on with the robbing and what not." He motioned his gun toward the window. "I don't do that anymore, Harlow."

"I know you got out. I understand. But this is different." She tried to ignore the tight feeling in her chest that appeared when he said her full name. It really wasn't helping her head.

"No, you don't understand, or else you wouldn't be here asking me for help."

"I don't need you for the whole thing. Just one part really." Harlow hadn't planned this properly, she realized that now. She had spent hours rehearsing what she was going to say to him, but, obviously, that should have been the first thing on her list.

"I don't want another job; I don't want another heist. Is it too much to ask you to come back in my life for coffee or dinner or something *legal*?"

"Is that a rhetorical question or—"

"Harlow!" He was pacing now, back and forth, still on the other side of the room.

"It's planned out. I planned it all out. I only need you for one small part, that's it. Just one, tiny, insignificant part, and then you can go back to..." She grimaced as she looked around. "Whatever this is."

"THIS," he waved his hands around, "is my life. A life I am proud to have built from the rubble YOU left behind." Regret filled him the moment he finished yelling. Those words, *his words*, could break Harlow. They always had that power.

"Can we not get into that now?" Lo closed her eyes and clutched her head desperately. Panic and fear and sadness soaked into her bones. She didn't want to think of any of that. She couldn't. It was a risk coming here; she wasn't strong enough, and she certainly wasn't ready yet.

Edward hesitated, seeing her standing there like a small bird blown off course by a storm miles away. She was frail but strong, capable of many things, this he knew. He had fallen in love with her, her intelligence, her wit, her ability to love beyond the point of insanity.

"I need help remembering..." Small tears fought their way out from behind her still-closed eyes.

"I told you. I don't do that anymore," his voice was weak. Everything had changed in his universe suddenly. The distant storm had unexpectedly changed course. One more plea, and she would begin to crack the wall he had worked so hard for so long to build up.

"Are you happy to see me?" the words tumbled out of her mouth before she could stop them.

Edward's body tensed up. Harlow rather wished she hadn't blurted out that question while he was holding a gun. He walked across the room toward her, not hesitating at all.

"You've no idea how happy I am to see you, Lo." He pulled her into a hug. Harlow didn't need to see his face to know he was crying.

Chapter Six

Seven years ago.

"Harlow, I wanted to speak with you for a moment," Dr. Tiproil quickly managed to catch the young girl before she slipped out of the classroom. She froze on the tips of her Chuck Taylors right on the threshold, chewing on her lip nervously as she turned around. Her attempts to conform and behave at university were beginning to look futile after the past few weeks. Most schools, she thought, would have appreciated someone with a high I.Q., but if you couple that with a loud mouth and a short temper, all you get is a bad reputation as a loose cannon and a know-it-all.

"Whatever it is, I can explain."

"I hope so…" He smiled slightly as he packed up his briefcase. His stern figure intimidated most students, but Harlow never seemed too bothered by it. Out of the corner of his eye, Tiproil could see her walking closer.

"Look, if it's about the almost fist fight with Dr. H that you broke up the other day, I just…I'm sorry you got involved, but he gave me a—"

"A grade you didn't deserve. I know." The professor closed his briefcase and studied Harlow for a moment before deciding to continue. "I spoke with him, and he agreed to change it to the grade you rightfully deserve."

Harlow hesitated for a moment, shifting her book bag from one shoulder to the other. "I…I didn't think it deserved an 'A,' but I don't get bad grades…" saying it out loud made Harlow cringe slightly. It sounded more arrogant than how she meant it. Maybe part of her reputation was well-earned.

"Now what I find odd," Dr. Tiproil continued, changing the topic, "is that someone actually broke into my office yesterday. Normally when students do this, they extract some type of revenge for a grade I've given them. But in this case, there was a thank-you card sitting on my desk."

"Do people not give you thank-you cards?" Harlow shrugged innocently.

"Not too many *students*, no." He chuckled. "And when they do give me cards, they don't do it illegally."

"Okay, I'm slightly confused. Are you mad about the card or the breaking-and-entering or that there was no property damage?"

"I'm not mad about any of those. I'm…I'm intrigued by you."

"Erm…thank you?"

It didn't take long for the friendship between Tiproil and Harlow to develop. Harlow would pop into Tiproil's office daily—both when he was present and when he was absent. She got into the habit of leaving him notes, since he enjoyed her thank-you card so much, she would leave him more. A note to say she hoped his day was going well, a note to explain how she 'found' the dean's fruit basket and was sure he'd want Tiproil to have it.

She didn't quite understand why this professor had taken a liking to her, but she knew she returned the feeling. They understood each other.

The weeks continued on, and Harlow knew they trusted each other completely. And that's when things changed.

Chapter Seven

Harlow sat on the couch, placing her now-empty beer bottle next to the overgrowing pile. Few words had passed between them in the past hour. She wondered how Edward was feeling. If it was anything like her own feelings, he would be ready to explode from a mixture of guilt, happiness, fear, sadness, and overwhelming nostalgia. Also a dash of excitement at what might happen. It was like the door to possibilities had been opened once more to them both. Harlow could feel the unused gears in her mind brush off the cobwebs and begin to work again, planning out heists and adventures, churning out schemes they could accomplish together. More banks to rob, museums to break into; she was sure Edward knew of some bad people with basic home security that they could break, enter, and thieve while feeling, for the most part, guiltless.

"I don't think I can help you," Edward's voice was a whisper, the noise from the T.V. almost washing it out entirely.

"I know you can. It'll be easy—"

"No, I'm too rusty. Too old. Hell, look at my alarm system; I thought it was good, until you proved otherwise."

"It *is* good; I'm just better." Harlow smiled, and so did Edward. "Besides, the front door wasn't an option; you aren't that rusty." They both took a sip of beer and let the T.V. groan on, neither paying attention to whatever program was playing but relieved there was something to distract them.

"It's a bank. It's easy. Just like we used to."

"You're able to do bank jobs on your own, Lo. You've even upgraded to prolific jewel heists too."

Harlow blushed, knowing Edward was referring to the latest jewel heist in the news which he obviously and correctly equated to her doing.

"I know you. Even if it's been a long time, I still know how your mind works." Edward felt his hands grow sweaty. He took another long sip of his beer. "So, if you need me, like you say, there's a damn good reason behind it."

Harlow reached into her pocket and pulled out two fake employee IDs. "I need this to be legitimate."

Edward help up one of the fake IDs with his picture on it. "Legitimate? I didn't know I was *legitimately* an employee of the Starr Bank Trust?"

"What I mean is, I can't have anyone knowing this job even took place." She snatched the ID back from his hand.

Edward finished off his beer, tossed it over with the others, and walked into the kitchen to grab a new one. He noticed Harlow's book bag sitting on the kitchen floor and curiosity took over. Carrying both the beer and the bag back out to the living room, he said, "Okay, lay it out for me."

Less than an hour later, Edward realized there was nothing about the plan he would change. It really was simple; he was hardly needed at all.

Smaller banks like Starr had smaller security systems which didn't necessarily make them easier to break into, but bypassing the security could be done on a smaller scale. Lo would cut part of the electrical line to the entire block; it would silence the bank alarms and security feed. Sadly, the locks were fed from a separate generator in case of such an event, but Harlow had thought of that too. Their fake employee ID cards she had gotten from a forger friend of hers would allow them to unlock the front door and walk right through, completely untraced. The map showed the outline of the bank was simple enough; no twisting corridors to get lost in, just a simple through the lobby, behind the counter, turn right, pick the lock on the second door, and walk right into the only room with safety-deposit boxes. Harlow already knew the number of the box and even had a key, although she wouldn't tell him who helped her make a copy. The tricky part was knowing the time it would take for the power outage to send out alerts to the bank owners and police. After some simple research on Google maps, Harlow had done the math to decipher response time. Unfortunately, there was a plus or minus three-minute difference she couldn't seem to work out, and three minutes meant the difference between success and failure. That was where Edward came in. Monitoring a simple police scanner allowed him to tell Lo how much time she had left until the police showed, and a simple live-stream camera three blocks away would allow him to tell Lo when a bank manager was on his/her way. The ability to get in and out before the shorter time of the two was unclear to Lo, and she didn't want to chance it; Edward couldn't argue that point. If anyone were coming, and she still wasn't out, he could simply create a delay.

The job was manageable with one person; easier with two. Still, there was something strange, something he couldn't quite put his finger on. Maybe it was why she specifically needed *him* to be the lookout, or where she had even gotten the idea for this heist to begin with. They sat in silence for what felt like forever, both going over the plan in their minds.

"So what is it with this one? What aren't you telling me? We never lie to each other, that was the one thing that kept us going for so long." (Lo's secret.)

Lo closed her eyes. Not only did he have a good memory, but Edward was smarter than he looked. She wasn't lying to him directly, of course he wouldn't see it that way. She did need him for the heist; that was partially true. But she also needed his memory for what came after. There were so many things she wanted to tell him, so many things she should tell him. But no matter what, he was already mixed up in this mess after all, and it was her fault. "Do you remember—?"

"Yes," he cut her off.

"Shut it." She shot him a fake-dirty look. It did bother her how he could remember everything. "When I left, we agreed there were some things that were going to happen, and when they did, we wouldn't tell each other about them. Not because we wanted to lie about anything, but just because ignorance is best sometimes." Edward nodded. Lo knew he understood instantly.

He leaned over and picked up the safety-deposit key from the coffee table. "This isn't a copy, is it? This is the one and only key to that box."

Lo nodded yes.

"It was a man who gave you the key, wasn't it?"

"We're not talking about it, Edward." She got up and began cleaning the pile of empty beer bottles. "If you want, we can do the heist early in the morning. I'll just need a few hours of sleep; I can be gone by tomorrow before the sun rises."

Was this what they had been reduced to? Edward wondered. They had been such a good team. But things were different now. "If that's what you think is best."

"It's time sensitive," Lo said from the kitchen. "I mean, obviously, every bank robbery is time sensitive, but the sooner I get what I need to, the better."

"I want to know what it is we're after." Edward stood in the doorway to the kitchen, staring at Lo who was staring at the tiles on the floor.

Lo was about to argue his use of the pronoun 'we' but decided against it. "Papers. Documents of a sort. Not valuable to many people, but to the right people, they're priceless." She looked up at him. "I really do like how you tiled these floors."

Chapter Eight

Margo looked over at the two men sitting in the empty cafe. They were drinking espresso and talking to each other in their native language which she, of course, understood. She would not have chosen either to work with her on this job, but her concerns were overridden. Georg had earned his place in the inner circle, and Leon...well, Leon needed to prove his worth. The ugly scar which ripped through his eyebrow marred his face as a constant reminder of his last mess-up. He had underestimated the security guard at the last robbery, allowing the man to fight back longer than necessary. Leon was slow and sloppy; the guard managed to use his own knife against him before Leon was able to kill him.

She turned back to focus her attention on making the phone call she was most dreading. They hadn't found what they were looking for. Tiproil was dead. Things were not going according to plan. Her boss would not be happy. Margo held the phone to her ear as it rang, hating having to report a failure, but that's what this was.

The national news was now beginning to pick up and sensationalize the Tiproil story; *Tiproil's Eden* was what they were calling it. *The man who knew the truth of our origin.* What a load of shit. The woman knew Tiproil had no idea the power he possessed with what he had discovered. He was too weak to know.

For months, they had worked to track down the information Tiproil possessed, spending thousands upon thousands of dollars to search down every avenue and leave no stone unturned. But Tiproil was smart enough to know how to avoid them; yes, he figured out quite quickly he wasn't the only one to know about the Garden of Eden, although he managed to keep his work a secret for quite some time.

Once he knew Margo and the rest were onto him, he agreed to do these series of press interviews. They gave him the publicity he wanted. He never thought Margo or her boss would risk going after him if it meant going into the spotlight. Well, he was wrong, and he had paid for his mistake with his life. But now, even in death, he was alluding them. They would have to find a way to get ahead of Tiproil.

Margo tensed as the voice on the other end spoke viciously at her. The anger was palpable, even through the airwaves.

"Yes, I saw the news story break. It is still late. Not many people are watching. They will not wake up from their sleep to listen about a man being shot."

Margo argued her case in her familiar language. The voice on the other line remained silent. "I am sorry. What do we do next?"

"He placed his trust in Harlow." The voice paused. "We should have seen this coming. They were still in contact. Find her. Get the key. Get me that information."

The phone went dead. Margo yelled at Leon and Georg, making them both jump slightly.

Leon spilled a bit of his espresso down his shirt.

"Clean yourselves up. We have a new job."

Harlow. The information on her was scarce and difficult to come by. Master thief, young, ambitious, and wickedly smart. That's almost as far as the intelligence went. She typically worked solo, although her network was vast, including men and women all over the world.

It didn't matter how difficult this job had become. They needed to get the key. It needed to be found. The world needed to know. Enough hiding and lying. The truth was out there, in plain sight, but people were too blind to see it. She would show them. They would all show them. Then, no one could ignore it anymore.

Chapter Nine

Six hours ago, he had been sitting on his couch, asleep, with beer to spare. Now, he was standing nervously in the lobby of the Starr Bank Trust, his eyes darting from the empty security monitors to the backdoor Lo had slipped through.

This was almost too easy, as the cliché went. But well-laid plans did make things easy.

Edward tried to relax.

"How's it going in there, Lo?" He looked down at his watch: three minutes remained until they entered the uncertain zone.

"Would be a lot better if you stopped asking me that every two seconds," her voice cracked its response through the Bluetooth attached to Edward's ear. He could hear the metal groaning of a box being pulled from its home.

"You're sure you carried the one when you did the calculation?"

"My math is spot on, Edward. Now shush." A thump followed by silence. The safety-deposit box was out, and Harlow was opening it.

He fought his urge to continue talking. Only one-and-a-half minutes left, assuming Harlow had done the math correctly. He had always been the one to run the numbers.

Being good at math wasn't secluded to someone with a memory as good as his, but Harlow's skills and attention had always been focused on other areas.

The inside of the bank was secure. He silently slipped through the side door and walked to their car, keeping his eyes peeled for any sign of cops or managers headed to assess the loss of power. The chilly night air helped him focus.

"You're in the gray zone," he said into his Bluetooth. "No sign of anything yet, but you need to get out of there as soon as you can. They could be here any minute."

No response from Harlow. Edward sighed; she hadn't changed much at all.

Without warning, a small sedan pulled onto a nearby street. Edward's muscles tensed up. He heard the ding of a mini alarm they had set up for this very purpose. The lonely car continued to drive toward the bank. Another warning beep.

"Harlow, we may have a problem." Edward moved silently toward the door of the bank.

There were parked cars across the street catty corner to theirs. A dog barking off in the distance.

A broken streetlight one block down. Another beep. The sedan continued to drive toward them.

"Lo. Lo, I think it's the manager. You need to get out." Still no response. The car was getting to the end of the block. Edward was going to have to create a diversion. "Dammit, Lo, this isn't fucking funny. Tell me you hear me. The manager is almost here."

He should get in the car and start it, wait for her to come outside. That was their plan. But he could feel it; something

44

was wrong. As stubborn as she was, Lo would never be silent like this. Her Bluetooth might have stopped working, and she wouldn't know she needed to leave A.S.A.P. or she could have fallen and hit her head. What if she twisted her ankle or broke a finger?

He needed to see her to know she was okay.

Turning away from the sedan, Edward ducked through the side door. His shoes made hushed, echoing clicks as he took long strides toward the backroom.

"Lo." His steps were cautious in the darkened hallway. "Lo, let's get a move on. You need to be—" Edward pushed the door open and felt his stomach drop. She was there, but she was not alone.

Silver boxes of various sizes with small numbers fastened to their front lined the walls. A large table sat in the center of the room used to hold the contents from the safety-deposit boxes. There was a small box opened on the table, its contents, which looked to Edward like old papers of some sort, were spread out. Nothing seemed too unusual except the people surrounding the table holding flashlights. Two large men twisting Harlow's arms behind her back, and one woman bent over the table, rapidly copying words into an open notebook.

"Oh shit," was all Edward could say. He needed to get Harlow, and he needed to get out.

"Edward!" Lo's face broke into a smile. She grimaced in pain as the two men holding her tightened their grip.

"I'm assuming these aren't friends of yours?" Edward felt himself instinctively reach for the gun strapped at his side. He knew whatever this situation was exactly, it was a ticking time bomb.

"Get the papers!" Harlow managed to yell only one order.

Outside the still-silent bank, the sedan pulled into the parking lot. The branch manager picked up his cellphone that started ringing on the dashboard. The second manager would be arriving in two minutes, and they would enter the building together, as was the bank's protocol.

No, nothing looked out of place. Probably just a normal power outage.

Everyone tried to speak at once, their voices clashing together after ricocheting off the metal-lined walls. Out of habit rather than necessity, no one raised their voice. Something about bank heists made everyone conscious of their voice levels.

"Let her the fuck go," Edward said.

"Who the fuck are you?" the woman writing in the journal asked.

Each goon holding Harlow mumbled in a language Edward couldn't understand. Harlow looked incredibly uncomfortable with her face now pushed against the table. Her eyes focused on nothing except the acid-worn papers in front of her.

"Lo…" Edward and the woman were staring at each other as if waiting to see who would make the first move. He could shoot the men and then the woman, but he seemed to think the woman herself might prove to be more deadly. Harlow still only stared at the papers.

"Don't wait. Take out your guns and shoot them!" the woman suddenly whispered. She moved to snatch up her notebook as the men pulled their guns and Edward did the same.

Four gunshots rang out, two hit their target, two missed. As Edward had predicted, the events unfolded almost too quickly for anyone to fully understand. They all reacted on pure instinct. The two men holding Harlow loosened their grip enough for her to shake them off. One went down, a gunshot through the side of his chest. The other somehow managed to send his bullet through the side of Edward's arm before ducking for cover beside his fallen comrade.

Out of the corner of his eye, Edward could see the woman snatching up her journal and sliding over the table, away from Harlow's reach.

He turned his gun toward her but, suddenly, heard the metallic clang of the safety-deposit box slamming into his gun. Edward yelled out in pain. His body collided with the woman's, and he found himself on the ground. The woman let the box clatter to the floor next to Edward's gun and his body as she ran for the hallway.

Harlow scrambled over the table in pursuit. The unwounded man reached up, his hand wrapping it around her ankle, causing her head to slam against the table mid-jump. The skin above her left eyebrow split, leaving a crimson-red smear where the safety-deposit box had been sitting. The old papers floated down to the ground, almost in slow motion, as if they had all the time in the world.

Edward felt something snap inside him at the sight. Ignoring the stinging from his arm, adrenaline coursed through his veins. From his spot on the floor, he picked up his fallen gun, aimed, and shot twice, the grunt and thump told him the man had fallen, but his concern was on Harlow.

He scanned the room once…twice…fuck. She was gone. "Lo!" He moved to stand up and run after her but remembered her only order. The papers. Whatever they had written on them, it was important enough for blood to be spilled.

Hurriedly, he collected the papers from all over the room, moving both of the men's bodies slightly to make sure he had them all. Knowing Harlow would be upset if any were torn, he tried his best to hold them gingerly as he sprinted out of the room after the women.

The lobby was still silent, as if unaware of the chaos that had just occurred inside its belly. Only Harlow stood there, panting for breath, looking around anxiously. Blood was running slowly into her eye, stinging terribly.

Suddenly, their watches beeped in unison.

"Lo, we need to go. We're out of time." Edward rushed over to where Harlow stood. The relief of seeing her mostly unharmed was like a tidal wave.

"She's gone...she has it...she's gone..." Edward grabbed Lo by the arm, ignoring her mumbling. He turned her to face him, noticing her eyes were wider than normal. "The papers," she muttered with her frizzy hair flying frantically around her face. "I need the papers."

"Lo, forget the papers, the managers—" but Harlow wouldn't let him finish. She struggled to throw his hands off her. "I have the papers! Lo, I have the papers!" He had to yell it twice for her to understand.

She calmed. Neither spoke. Edward pushed the slightly crumpled pile into her shaking hands, and they quickly walked out of the side door.

"We need to drop the car somewhere. It's only a matter of time before someone puts two and two together." They climbed in the car and drove off, waiting a block before turning on the headlights. "So much for in and out undetected. Dead men in the safety-deposit room. Well, it's not so safe after all." Edward looked over from the driver's seat. Lo was barely listening, worried only about the papers on her lap.

"Are any missing?"

"No. They're all there." Lo closed her eyes in relief and exhaustion.

Edward turned the wheel; he was heading for the closest underpass. The highway would be somewhat busy, but underneath the bridge, they could drop the car off and no one would be the wiser this time of night. Harlow's hands were still shaking.

"Hey, we got the papers." He knew she was about to cry. "Everything's okay, the job was kind of...messy...but we got what we came for."

"It's not okay." Her eyes were still closed.

"We got out of there, mostly unharmed."

"It's not okay."

"We'll be okay."

"No, we won't!" Harlow found herself yelling. "You have no idea what just happened!"

"I was in the room! I have eyes! You've been back in my life for less than 24 hours, and I'm getting shot at!" He waved his bloody arm in the air.

"Oh, would you relax? I'm not the one who shot you."

"Is that supposed to make me feel better?!" Edward's voice went up an octave. He turned the car down a gravel road, slowing slightly as the rocks clinked against the underbelly.

"You don't understand! You don't understand what this means." She lifted up the papers.

"Then why don't you tell me what I got shot over!? Not to mention half the bones in my hand are probably broken."

"Pull over here; we'll get rid of the car." Harlow ignored his comments.

Edward did as he was told, but grudgingly so.

"Is it traceable?" Harlow asked.

"No," he responded. The car doors thudded shut silently, the two of them standing outside in the chilly air. "Pieced together. VIN and license plate match, so it won't raise too many alarms, but it's not in my name."

"I thought you got out of this business." Harlow smirked. She held the papers close to her chest.

"Old habits." He shrugged. Edward went about prepping the car for burning it, syphoning the gas out of the tank and spilling it over the cloth seats. It took only a few minutes. Harlow was silent, looking something up on her phone.

"Ready to get warm?" Edward asked.

"Can I do it?" she asked with an alarming amount of enthusiasm.

"Sure." He handed her the flare, trying to hide a smile. She hesitated for a moment, then handed him the papers gently. Turning toward the car, she lit the flare and threw it in the open window. The dark night turned to light as the gasoline ignited.

This wasn't quite how Edward had envisioned his night going, but whenever Harlow was in your life, nothing was predictable. He looked away from the growing flames, over at the woman he had fallen desperately in love with.

"Your head is bleeding still." His hands reached over instinctively, gently brushing her hair away from the angry, red wound.

"It'll stop soon. Just hope I don't have a scar." Her comment suddenly reminded them both of the men, their bodies probably being found by the managers right about now.

"We should get going." She took the papers back from Edward's hands.

"It's a long walk."

"That's why I made arrangements." She held up her phone.

"You better not have called an Uber."

"Relax. I contacted a friend."

"Who did you...?" Edward froze. "You didn't. Harlow...you didn't call her."

Chapter Ten

Seven years ago.

Tiproil stared out at the snow as he finished his lecture. It had been a week since he'd decided he would tell Harlow the truth. It was years before he found a student he thought he could trust, a student who valued education enough to understand the gravity of what he had, and a student special enough to do what needed to be done. Now was the time— Harlow would help him and become the one, or she would leave, like so many before had done.

Christmas decorations sprung up around campus, red bows plastered on almost every door, including Dr. Tiproil's. It managed to survive three days before he tore it down; it was the principal of the matter, he told Harlow. The school thought they could just do anything they wanted to people's doors, force them into the Christmas spirit. Of course, in the spirit of Christmas, Tiproil offered the bow for Harlow to take home. Naturally, she accepted the contraband and smuggled it off campus that day.

The snow continued to fall, and Harlow was waiting patiently in Tiproil's office for him to get done with class; he still locked his door, but he was no longer surprised to open it at any hour and see Harlow sitting in a chair inside.

She liked the quiet calm of his office, the way it smelled like ink and tangerines.

She had studied the entire room over and over again, to the point where she was beginning to have the layout of his books committed to memory. She'd borrowed a good third of them already. There was one space she'd never looked though, one space Tiproil had never opened with her around. It was beginning to get to her, like a crooked picture hanging on a wall. She would see it and want to fix it, but she couldn't quite reach it. Every drawer in his desk had been opened at some point over the past semester, for a pen or some paper; all the file cabinets noisily yanked open from their squeaky places too. Finally, she could resist it no longer. She knelt down and, in 30 seconds, had the lock picked and the doors open.

She wasn't too sure what she was staring at. A half-pint bottle of black-label whiskey sat toward the front; papers, folders, journals, and books that were piled up behind it. Why were they hidden? The whiskey made sense, but these papers?

"I was wondering how long it would take you to find that. The curiosity must've been killing you." Tiproil stood in the doorway, a slight frown on his face.

"I'm sorry!" Harlow almost fell backward as she tried to jump away. "It was just...I'd never seen it and..."

"It's all right." Tiproil turned around and locked his office door. Harlow bit her lip, still sitting on the ground. She watched him calmly walk over to his chair, taking off his coat and tossing it on the coat rack in the corner as he went. "Did you get a chance to look through any of it?"

Harlow shook her head no, knowing it was definitely *not* all right.

He bent down and pulled out the bottle of whiskey. Hesitating for a moment, he handed the bottle to Harlow.

"Take a swig." She did as he instructed. He took the bottle back and took a swig himself. "I want you to take this." Papers slid out of their place from the shelf as Tiproil rummaged around, trying to find one file in particular. "Read it as soon as you can. Then...well, I need it back, so return it when you're done."

Harlow held the folder in her hands tightly. She wanted to apologize again but knew, at this point, it was better to take her strange gift and go. Tiproil wasn't in the mood for her antics today. She wished him a Merry Christmas, unlocked the door, closed it behind her, and walked down the hallway.

The snow was flying, and she almost lost her footing twice on the walk to her off-campus apartment. Inside the dry and mostly warm safety of her bedroom, she opened the folder. It took her four hours to read the entire contents; Harlow didn't sleep at all until she had read every last word twice. The snow was finally slowing outside in the dark when she curled up under her blankets and began to doze off. The folder laid gently on the top of her bookshelf which doubled as a nightstand. The very top of a paper stuck out, its bold letters visible in the dim light. They read: 'Garden of Eden,' and Harlow knew she had just opened the proverbial Pandora's Box.

Chapter Eleven

"Jane is a friend, even if you act like she isn't. She's going to come help us."

Edward marched ahead of Harlow in total silence, his anger permeating through the early morning air. Harlow trailed along behind, talking incessantly, knowing Edward could hear her.

Harlow's exploits into the underground world introduced her to many people—including Jane. Jane had been one of the first of Harlow's friends Edward had ever met. Years ago, when they first began working together, Harlow introduced the two of them to each other. Neither liked the other, and not for any particular reason, but the source of their hate certainly never prevented it from flourishing.

Jane couldn't have cared any less that Edward had a super-powered brain, she thought he was selfish, idiotic, and much too old for Harlow, and she constantly reminded both of them.

A short and charming blonde-haired, blue-eyed beauty, Jane was the last thing anyone would expect to do what she did, including Edward.

"Listen, I know the job didn't go exactly as planned, but all things considered, I have the papers I needed and you...well, you haven't been identified. Sure, the cops are probably looking at the dead bodies right now, and, yeah, I guess your gun will be linked to the bullets in their bodies, but whatever. You can report it stolen." She had to hurry to keep up with him and was beginning to run out of breath with all the talking she continued to do. "You've got no connection to the murders—"

"Other than my gun being the murder weapon?" Edward snapped back at her, not bothering to turn around.

"Oh, yeah, okay, other than that...Edward, why are you walking so quickly? I told you, we'll have a ride soon enough."

"If you think I'm getting in a car with her, you are more insane than ever before."

"Oh, don't be such a drama queen." Lo rolled her eyes. The dried blood felt odd against her skin, and the cut above her eyebrow still stung. "Where are you going anyway?"

"Home."

"What?" She looked around the streets of the suburb they had been walking in for the past few minutes.

"Home, it's a building with my bed in it. A bed I sorely need." He continued on, their footsteps the only noise to be heard. "And we can get your head looked at."

"But we can't go back home. Those people—"

"I have work tomorrow," was his only reply.

"Oh, for crying out loud. Can't you take off the day after a heist?"

"Yes, Harlow, let me phone my boss quickly and explain to them why I need to take a day off. Just too busy robbing a bank and shooting two men, and I might have a concussion. Oh, also, I forgot to mention I had to set my car ON FIRE, so the bus is my only option now!" He was facing her now, his breathing had quickened.

"Sounds legitimate enough to me." Harlow shrugged.

Edward threw his hands up in frustration and carried on, turning down another side street.

Harlow hated the suburbs for this reason; all the houses looked too similar, especially in the dark.

The only way to get around was by memorizing the street names which was incredibly tedious. On more than one occasion, Harlow had to fight the urge to rearrange the green signs in the middle of the night; a prank Jane had put her up to long ago. She smiled at this memory and looked for the nearest street sign out of curiosity.

"Chestnut Street…Edward, at this rate, we'll be home"

"In three blocks, yes."

Harlow kept her mouth shut for the remainder of those three blocks. She took out her phone and sent a short message to Jane, informing her friend that her shuttle services would no longer be needed. At least Edward's house would be safe; they hadn't been followed and had covered their trail enough for the next few days. They could both get some rest before the real work began. Of course, Edward was unaware that he might even be involved in any of this next stage; Harlow knew she should mention something to him, but the timing wasn't right just yet.

They walked in through the backdoor; Edward explaining how the security was easier to deactivate from the back. Harlow managed not to make an inappropriate joke.

"I'll get you blankets; you can crash on the couch until later. I want you out by noon, do you understand?"

"Yeah." She yawned and took off her black jacket and sneakers, too tired to protest. Her hands were stiff from holding the papers for so long, but, even now, she refused to let them out of her clutches. She contemplated taking off her dark jeans since they were filthy, but decided against leaving them by the backdoor in the kitchen. "I really do like this tile."

Edward rolled his eyes and went about resetting his home-security system. "Flattery won't get you out of answering any questions I have."

"Worth a shot," she mumbled. "Could we at least get a few hours of sleep before the debriefing?"

"I told you, I have work tomorrow."

Harlow raised an eyebrow at the strangeness of his sentence. The alarm beeped three times, alerting them that it had been successfully reactivated.

"Fine. I call off tomorrow. But that's it! Only so you can explain what's happening and then leave. We can say goodbye properly and make sure I'm not a target of any investigation."

Less than ten minutes later, Harlow was curled up in Edward's bed, curly hair flung around her face on one of his pillows, and her dark body wearing one of his old t-shirts. He had protested to her sleeping in his bed, as he was also planning to sleep there, but, in the end, she won out. No surprise to Edward; Harlow still managed to get what she wanted.

He laid still under the covers, listening to the familiar sound of her breathing and realized how much he had missed her. Maybe there was something to be said about her coming back into his life now. After all, things were different. They had both changed. Well, kind of.

The stolen papers lay gently on the nightstand beside her. He reached over, unable to stop himself, and began to look through them, the light from the streetlamps illuminating enough of the pages.

"Edward," her voice was a whisper, almost lost to the night.

He grunted in response, not realizing he had dozed off. The papers lay scattered around the covers on the bed. In their sleep, both Edward and Harlow had moved next to each other.

"Some people may or may not want me dead." Harlow felt the urge to point out the obvious, having woken suddenly with only that thought on her mind.

"I told you this was a bad idea, Lo," he mumbled, still half asleep.

Harlow rolled over to face him, suddenly alert. "Okay, firstly, you had no idea I was showing up, and, secondly, how would I have any control over this situation?"

"Don't you give me that shit." It was Edward's turn to roll over so he could face Harlow. "You show up here, after...after everything, and I'm supposed to what, just assume nothing chaotic is going to happen? I'm just trying to have a nine-to-five life."

"You and I aren't made for a nine-to-five life. We know that."

"Who were those people, Lo?" Edward changed the subject.

"What people?"

Edward rolled his eyes. "The only people we met tonight, Lo. The angry, gun-wielding thieves in the bank."

"Oh, well, I don't know them personally."

"Obviously they weren't there because they wanted to bake Christmas cookies with you. How do you know the two men I shot?"

"I don't know them! They could just be mercenaries sent to do someone else's business!"

"Are you trying to tell me it was just a coincidence that the same night we break into a bank, someone else was doing just that? And they were after the same exact thing we were?"

"I told you; those papers were valuable."

"Valuable enough for two men to die," he muttered to himself. These days, he tried not to think about anyone who had died, especially those at the hands of his own gun. He had killed before, so the initial shock was absent, but it still shook him every time he took a life. At least these men had been shooting back. "What about the woman? You must have some idea where she's headed?"

"Some idea, yeah." Harlow looked down at the stolen papers, picking one up. She smiled softly. She had known Edward would read the papers. He couldn't resist. "That woman, she got more information than she ever should have. She copied some of it down in her journal before you got there."

Edward nodded, not fully understanding just yet. "I won't ask you to tell me too much more, but, Lo, there are key facts I need to know here."

"I know." She swallowed the lump in her throat. "Someone...someone hid something valuable, and this is the first clue as to where they hid it."

"And those people, they now have part of this first clue."

She nodded. "Even *part* is bad. I was supposed to have this before anyone could ever see any of it."

"But what is it?" Picking up a paper, he studied the numbers scrawled across the aging surface. The curiosity was burning inside him; he wanted to know what two men had died over, what he had killed over.

Harlow never had a chance to answer the question; a strange scratching came suddenly from downstairs as Edward's alarms began to go off.

Chapter Twelve

Seven years ago.

Harlow had run back the next day, breathless and filled with questions, only to find the office empty. Tiproil was reluctant to answer all of them and kept many of his correspondence cryptic until their meeting today. The less she knew, the better, but she could tell: he wanted her to know. It was too difficult to keep going on his own, impossible even. Including someone younger and clever like Harlow would make his undertaking a success.

"Harlow, if I told you it was all true, everything written, what would you say?"

"I'd say that you're crazy. It's impossible for so many reasons…" Harlow let her voice trail off as she sat down cautiously in the old chair that barely fit in the room. She knew the look Tiproil had painted on his face right now; it was one of patronizing patience. The look he gave smart students when they needed a moment to grasp a gap in logic to come to the correct conclusion.

"The Garden of Eden is a real place." Tiproil's body relaxed, as if he had waited for a long time to finally say those words out loud to someone who might believe them.

"No. That's impossible," Harlow argued immediately. Despite all she had read, her mind still could not fully process an idea such as this. "How does that even work? If the Garden of Eden were real, we would be talking about the beginning of creation. We have rock samples that date the earth at over four-billion years old. The fossil record tells us evolution was a long path with dead ends...look at the trail of hominids! We can literally trace the line of evolution back to something that doesn't even resemble mankind. How could you possibly say there was a literal Adam and Eve who started all of creation?"

"You can't take everything in the Bible verbatim. Widen your view, Harlow. We know there is a Mitochondrial Eve—a female whose mDNA is the same as all of humanity's, the mDNA in all of us can be traced back to her. Is it more difficult to suppose there is some type of Adam too who's partial DNA we all share?"

"No, I guess not." Harlow picked at a loose seam in the chair cushion. This was all so much to take in. "But we're talking about the dawn of humanity. The first archaic Homo sapiens..."

"Which explains the fossil record showing other hominids. They existed too. What's more difficult for me to believe is that out of all those genetic quirks and twists and turns, somehow mankind managed to emerge *without* any type of help."

"A divine hand helping evolution along? How very progressive of you."

"Even the Catholic Church agrees there was some type of big bang. Science and religion, or science and God rather, *do* go hand in hand."

"But then we're looking for some type of hunter-gatherer society, right? Cave dwellers who struggled to communicate and…" Harlow's mind was spinning. The cushion's thread became close to unraveling. "Societies that old…all that's left of them are things like cave paintings and rock shelters. An odd skull or two solidified in a lucky landslide. And, somehow, Eden fits into all of this?"

"Think about the descriptions of Eden—a paradise with domestic animals and plants giving food constantly. If what the Bible says is true, Eden would have been a location our ancestors could thrive in. They wouldn't have to worry about hunting and gathering or about droughts or floods or starvation of any kind."

"You mean agriculture? Like the agricultural revolution that began the Neolithic Revolution?" He nodded yes. "Tiproil, you're contradicting yourself. Some of the earliest remains of our ancestors are over 100,000 years ago. If you want to talk about domestication…that type of thing didn't start until 10,000 years ago. There's a massive gap there."

"You can't think so literally, Harlow! Perhaps it's where they first began to find successful agricultural tendencies like domestication of plants and animals. It would have been revered as holy by everyone."

"So…what happened to it?"

"I believe the Garden of Eden is some type of ceremonial place the first Homo sapiens built and worshiped in. Hunter-gatherer societies didn't have cities. I also believe something happened that caused them to flee from it and God to block it off from anyone ever finding it."

"But why? If it's a legitimate place, then you can't honestly believe there is some type of supernatural power hidden there."

"That's a story for tomorrow, Harlow." Tiproil knew to be cautious. If he overloaded Harlow with information, she might run away. He had already told her so much.

"So it all could be real." Harlow proved to be more open to the possibility than he had initially hoped.

"And, as for now, I have a class to teach. And you have one shortly you need to be in as well I believe."

Harlow rolled her eyes but grudgingly agreed to leave. She handed back the crumpled papers, a million questions still on her mind.

"How did you find out about Eden?" She couldn't hold it back. She wanted to know.

"Another story for another day." He rose out of his chair and stretched. It was time to go.

Chapter Thirteen

Harlow and Edward both flopped out of bed in the least graceful way imaginable, snatching up the stolen papers as quickly as they could and stacking them into one crumpled pile.

"Fuck. I could've sworn we weren't followed," Harlow spoke quickly as she pulled pants and socks on, narrowly avoiding toppling onto the bedroom floor.

"Hell, two of the three people are dead," Edward added from the floor where he sat to put his shoes on while scanning through the security footage linked to his phone. "The noise sounded like it was coming from the back of the house...back bathroom window."

They both darted down the steps, taking them two at a time. Harlow had to follow Edward into the kitchen, as she couldn't fit alongside him through the doorway. Her hands began to sweat, clutching the stolen papers, but she didn't once think of setting them down.

It was difficult to see around Edward's broad shoulders, even if she and he were the same size height-wise. The doorway to the half-bath off the kitchen was even smaller than the one they had just come through, and Harlow stood on her tiptoes to see.

A head full of platinum-blonde hair was clamoring through the window above the toilet which still had its seat up.

"Jane?" Harlow asked, knowing already who the woman was.

"Why the hell are you climbing in through my bathroom window?" Edward's question was less tactful.

"Well." She grunted as she stepped down onto the toilet then onto the floor. "The front door wasn't an option."

Edward held up a very angrily pointed finger back and forth from Lo to Jane. "Why is it you two ladies insist on using windows to enter my home?"

"She just said, the front door—"

"It's not going to ever be an option because I'm going to cement over it as soon as you both leave!" Edward stopped Harlow mid-sentence.

"But then we would be *forced* to climb in through a window," Jane pondered aloud.

Edward threw his hands in the air and walked into his kitchen, allowing Harlow to slip through and give Jane a hug.

"I told you not to come!" She began rambling right away. "Thank you so much....but we managed to get back without any issues and...well, you certainly made an entrance with the alarms. I thought you'd be able to beat them. I was able to."

The women moved into the kitchen with Edward. Jane gave a puzzled look. "I didn't set off any alarms."

No sooner had the words left her mouth than there was a knock at the front door.

"Did someone just hear a knock?" Edward froze. Eyes wide, all three of the criminals looked from face to face, searching for an answer to who was at the door, who had set off the security alarms, and who would be standing there, knocking.

The noise came again. Edward and Harlow stood behind the kitchen island in the same spot they had been the night before. It felt like a lifetime ago when, in reality, the only thing that had passed was a heist and two deaths. That was always the problem with those two: two years apart felt like two minutes, and two days together could feel like a lifetime.

The knock came again and the pair tensed; Harlow didn't notice her hand reflexively reach for Edward's. Jane suddenly popped back into the room, walking to stand with the duo behind the kitchen island. She took a deep breath and ignored noticing how Edward took a step back to separate himself from Harlow.

"What is it?" Harlow whispered, waiting in the tense silence for what she hoped was a good answer. There was no way they had been followed back from the heist.

"I forgot I ordered pizza," Jane whispered back.

"Wha—" Both Edward and Harlow began to voice their arguments at her lack in judgment.

"I'm kidding!" The blonde grabbed a gun from her hip.

"Who the hell is at my front door?" Edward snapped.

"Judging from their black clothes and guns, I'd say some men who want you dead." Jane took the hand not holding her pistol and used it to tuck a piece of stray hair behind her ear. "Can I go take care of them?"

"What, shoot them on my front porch? Absolutely not. I want to be able to come back to this neighborhood," Edward protested.

"Fine." Jane holstered her gun with an audible harrumph. "You suburban people. I will never understand you."

"We're going out the back." Edward ignored her. He looked over to make sure Harlow was listening as she collected the precious papers. He turned back to Jane. "And if things need to get messy...as long as it's in the backyard, Jane. With some type of plausible deniability for me."

She pulled out her gun again, and a smile stretched across her face, giving Edward a pinch of concern. Jane was, after all, an assassin.

Another knock on the front door pulled him from his reservations about Harlow's friend. Each knock seemed to be growing in intensity, like bullets smashing through closer and closer to their mark. Edward knew it was only a matter of time before bullets were, in fact, smashing through his front door. He almost wished they would have just broken in through a window.

Jane left first, assessing the backyard before cracking the door and creeping through it into the night. Edward crouched to the same level Jane had been at and moved to follow her, but Harlow's arm reached out and stopped him.

"Edward...wait." She pulled him away from the door, closer to her body. "I...I think I'm in a bit of trouble." It was painful for her to admit.

Edward took a breath. This really wasn't the best time for her to begin to share her feelings. "I know, Harlow."

"What?" She paused, her brows furrowing together in typical Harlow fashion. "You know? How?"

"Just because we haven't talked doesn't mean I'm not keeping an eye on you," he commented sheepishly. "But also, the mercenaries outside my door are a dead giveaway."

"Firstly, I said they MIGHT be mercenaries, and, secondly—"

"No, absolutely not. You aren't allowed to discuss technicalities when there are gunmen involved."

"If you two are done bickering, I do believe our house guests are ready to enter," Jane's voice hissed through the door.

"Lo," Edward turned back around, but his final words were interrupted by another knock, this time followed by a muffled voice. "They're getting ready to enter."

Harlow spoke not a word and turned on her heel, fidgeting with the tile Edward had so nicely placed on the ground. At the front door, there was a loud bang, followed by shouting and calling by names no one understood.

The cold metal from a large M-16 pushed against his hand shocked Edward's gaze from the noises back to Harlow. She was lying on her stomach, leaning down into a small pit hidden underneath tiles that were now piled to the side.

"How did you know I had a stash of M-16s hidden down there?" He was shocked.

"Since when do you tile anything yourself?" Harlow looked up with a matter-of-fact grin. "I know you, Edward."

With a wink and a nod, she crawled out of sight, an extra M-16 for Jane clenched tightly in her hands. Edward wasted only a second before hastily moving after her; he didn't want to be the only one left behind when the mercenaries moved to the kitchen.

Chapter Fourteen

The streets grew easier to see as the strange trio of an assassin, a thief, and a reformed thief-turned-retail-manager sped away in the assassin's car from a gang of unconfirmed, possible mercenaries. No one knew quite where to go, but they knew they needed to go, and quickly. With luck and good timing, the possible mercenaries had been too slow to follow; Harlow's theory was they wanted to search the house thoroughly before checking the roads. It seemed just as likely as all the other theories flying through the air, except perhaps Jane's third theory in which the mercenaries were enthusiastic and overly zealous Jehovah's Witnesses.

In the rush to climb into the car, Harlow and Edward had somehow both ended up in the backseat with Jane driving. Since there was no possibility of stopping, Harlow began to climb to the open front seat as Jane zipped down the empty highway.

"I still say we go to the university," she suggested again with her upper half successfully into the passenger seat.

"No." Edward was adamant. "And I told you to put your feet first." His hands tried in vain to protect his face from her flailing feet.

"I can get us into the library without any trouble." She grunted, tugging to no avail.

"No."

"I know people…people who will be willing to." Harlow's upper body slid under the glove compartment while her feet shot up toward the roof of the car.

"Help?" Jane suggested.

"No, Harlow." Edward took ahold of her feet and slid them gently above the armrest while reaching his hand out to lift her up. "We need another place to go."

"Oh Lord. You…you're not still jealous of him, are you?" Harlow paused, her hand still holding onto Edward's.

"Lo…" he growled. She knew she was entering dangerous territory.

"I know a place." Jane sensed the hostility and ended it before the conversation could gain any more traction.

"Good. Now, we need to figure out who those people were." Edward pulled out his phone and brought his security footage up on the screen. Jane and Harlow exchanged looks from the front.

Trying to find out who the bad guys are; *They spoke German?*

"I thought I heard the name 'Margo,' but I could be wrong."

Margo has a journal with the first few steps written down. "We have to figure it out before she does." Harlow is focused on the papers, not the conversation. "What do you think this symbol is?"

"Which page?" Edward asked without looking up.

"First one, halfway down. Could be a man holding a fish?"

"It's a man next to a hut."

Harlow flipped the paper, turned her head, and nodded in agreement.

"I almost forgot about your superpower, Edward," Jane said smugly.

"Not a superpower. Not even that interesting." He squinted closer at his screen. "Son of a bitch! They're smashing the tiles in the kitchen!" Harlow bit her lip.

"NO! NOT THE GAZEBO OUT BACK!" Edward seemed to forget his voice couldn't be heard through the phone.

"Well, whoever they are, they're committed to destruction, that's for sure."

"Jane, I apologize."

"For...?"

"Not letting you shoot them on my front porch. The damned homeowners association will never let me rebuild that gazebo." He turned off his phone and tossed it onto the empty seat beside him.

"Since when do you give a shit about gazebos?" Harlow turned around quizzically.

"We're here." Jane pulled the car to a stop as the sun finished coming over the horizon. The sky was still pink and purple, not quite transformed to its usual blue. The neon sign '24-HOUR FITNESS' shone aggressively to the trio in the car.

"A gym?" Harlow looked as if Jane had lost her mind. A few early risers walked past the parked car and entered the building.

"The last place they would expect us to take priceless, ancient..." Jane hesitated. "What exactly are they after?"

"Assuming they aren't sent by the homeowners association to ruin my home, they're after some papers we stole," Edward said bitterly from the backseat.

"Cheer up, Edward." Lo shut the car door quietly and watched him get out from the backseat. "We're going to figure it all out and get you your gazebo back."

Edward's mumbles were inaudible over the cling of the door opening. The gym was surprisingly alive for such an early hour, comprised mostly of what looked to be businessmen and women, dedicated to achieving their fitness goals before work. Jane, who had obviously been here before, led the group over to a small cafe area where she ordered three smoothies and sat down.

"Best smoothies in town."

"Why are you the way that you are?" Ed shook his head at Jane.

"The papers." Harlow quickly pulled the folder onto the table, changing the subject before the two could get into an argument. "The papers aren't as old as you think. If my research is correct, we're looking at maybe 400 years or so."

"Not that old?" Edward raised an eyebrow.

"She liked your wrinkly ass, and that's about how old you are," Jane snapped.

"The author is unknown, but I have my suspicions as to who it was." Harlow continued on ignoring them both. "They were copied from the actual original text made sometime around 1000 A.D. Some context for you, Edward, that's after the Roman Empire but before the Renaissance."

"Thank you, but none of that makes any of this more clear to me, because I don't know what any of those words mean."

"Thank you for your honesty." She sighed. "Well skipping the history lesson then—"

At that moment, an exhausted teenager slapped the three smoothies Jane had ordered down on the table. "Three Mean Green's. If you don't like them, we don't want to hear about it."

"That is *awful* customer service." Ed gawked, but the teen had already left.

"Doesn't matter, these are delicious." Jane handed the smoothies around the table while simultaneously slurping hers.

"Can we focus, please?" Harlow pushed her smoothie away, annoyed. "Long story short, if this is what I think it is…well, they're a code that will give us directions of some sort." Her words were met with slurping noises. "Did none of you hear what I just said? Directions…ancient clues…history…secrets? Anything?"

"Wud do dey pud en ere?" Edward asked, the straw still in his mouth.

"Dunno, bud dey good," Jane responded with the same straw/smoothie garbled voice.

Harlow's angry gaze made them both come up for air and sit silently, ready for her to continue on with her story.

"Edward, you and I were stealing these to keep them out of the hands of bad people. Ever since I first learned of these, I knew others were after them too. I think it was those people who came after us and…destroyed your gazebo."

"Please tell me this isn't one of your treasure hunts," Ed asked sincerely. "No, not another historical mystery that got my house destroyed this time. Harlow! Why didn't you start with this before the heist?"

"It doesn't matter! Because you would have agreed to help me even if you knew the homeowners association would blacklist you for all eternity. This is more important than anything like that." They could tell Harlow was worried, and not just about the historical value these papers had. This was real fear.

"I wasn't going to say anything, but...well, you two have a right to know now that you're mixed up in this.

"The stories in the Bible are loosely based in historical fact. We all know this, even historians who are Christian, Jewish, Islamic, Atheist; they all agree that there is historical validity in parts of the Bible. For example, we know Jesus was in fact a real person who was crucified by the Romans in the time of Augustus. You can't deny that; now what people don't agree on is how valid all of the stories are in terms of verbatim legitimacy. Do you take the words literal or are some of them figurative? Is the earth only 6,000 years old? Well, we have proof that says definitely not, but some people still insist it is because the Bible says so.

"I'm not about to launch into a debate over the infallibility of one of the holiest books in the world. But what I am going to say is...I know for a fact most of the places are real...including the Garden of Eden, and these papers are the first step to finding it. I didn't believe it at first; it seemed too far-fetched. Like something out of Indiana Jones, but the more I looked into it, the clearer it all became."

"It wasn't just you," Edward's voice was soft.

"No." Lo shook her head. "Dr. Tiproil who works at my old university stumbled onto this long before I came on the scene."

"I watched his interviews on T.V. They were really convincing," Jane said.

"Convincing because they're true." Edward understood that much. He had watched the interviews like so many around the world, eyes glued to the screen, unable to deny every question, and doubt having a solid answer. "Now that your precious professor spilled the beans on national T.V., I'd say the whole damn world knows about Eden."

"His interviews set off a global phenomenon if you will." Harlow bit her lip as she ignored Edward's cutting comment. "Groups from all around the world began contacting him, discussing their hunt for the Garden. It isn't a secret anymore, and people are determined to find the Garden of Eden. This cypher contains instructions on where to find the first step on the path to the Garden. Well, I guess, technically, this would be the first step," she motioned to the papers, "and what comes next would be the second. But you get the idea. Since we have the only copy, I normally wouldn't be too concerned about decoding it except…"

"Except these mysterious bad guys wrote down part of it already," Edward finished her sentence. "So we don't have the only copy."

"How much did they write down?" Jane asked. It was beginning to become clear to her all that she had missed during the heist.

"We don't know. They had me held down at an awkward angle. There were at least three solid minutes of uninterrupted writing. All I know is we can't risk them getting on the trail. From what I understand, the first page links to the first location and then that location will guide you to another. I don't know how many locations there are or what the rest of these pages are used for. I only know we have to get there before these people do."

The trio sat in silence with the only noises coming from the various exercise equipment. The gravity of the situation began to sink in. They may never know the group of people that broke into Edward's home and ruined his standing with the homeowners association. They might never fully understand who the group in the bank heist were either. Perhaps the groups had no knowledge of each other. With the professor's interviews being cast across the world, it was perfectly plausible there were ten or 15 other gangs ready to descend upon them.

"We have to protect whatever this leads to," Edward's words were simple, but the trio understood their magnitude and complexity.

Chapter Fifteen

Edward was the first to ask a question.

"How do we decipher it? I know those pages without even looking at them, Lo. They're gibberish. I can write them down a thousand times, but we won't understand them at all."

"I know. I've looked through the pages too. It's…complicated. Tiproil and I had worked it down to two possibilities, well, one really. The pictures are representations to chapters, and the numbers correspond to specific sentences, words, and letters."

"None of these look like words. They're just letters." Jane tilted her head to the side.

"That's what all words are, Jane. The same 26 letters rearranged." Harlow set down her phone and looked over at Jane's writing. "Or in this case, 23 letters."

"I'm assuming that means something to you, because it means nothing to us." Ed still held the papers gently in his hands.

"It's in Latin."

"Of course." Ed was sarcastic.

"English didn't begin to pick up until around the 11th century. Before then, it was Old English which was introduced—"

"We get it, Nerd. It's in Latin. Unfortunately, my Latin is a bit rusty." Jane sighed.

"So is mine." Lo bit her lip. "But Google's isn't." She held up her phone triumphantly.

Harlow busied herself, typing the Latin words into Google Translate while the other two sat quietly, thinking. Edward couldn't help but replay the events of the heist in his mind.

"Margo…they called her by her name, Margo. The woman writing down the symbols in her journal is named Margo." Edward smiled, proud of himself. The Mean Green smoothies had been forgotten about completely.

"That's a start. What about language, were they speaking English?" Jane asked.

"No, it sounded like German? Maybe?"

"Done," Lo interrupted their train of thought.

The head with three empty tombs.
She built her cross with garden above.
Her tomb she built, body not below.
The eternal city for the emperor's sister.
The garden grows in the light for the woman seated in her throne.

"Probably could've just kept it in the Latin," Ed joked.

Harlow said nothing but bit her lip and furrowed her eyebrows together in thought. If only Tiproil were here; he would know what this was referring to; he would understand it. She knew he would. But for all his knowledge, where had it gotten him? Tiproil was dead. She had helped kill him accidentally. The people who killed him were coming after her. They threatened to destroy every precaution she and Tiproil had ever taken.

"Let me talk it out. Drink your smoothies." Neither protested Harlow's orders. "A 'head with three empty tombs' that could be anything. The number three is all over the Bible. Three days in the tomb before resurrection, three parts in the Holy Trinity. What about 'Garden above'; who puts a garden above? Above what? Above ground? All gardens are above ground, it's the roots that are below. I guess, if you're drying out herbs, you hang them from the ceiling, and, in that case, the plants are dead…but that isn't a tomb…"

"The tomb is empty," Jane offered. "It says, 'her tomb she built body not below,' so we're looking for an empty tomb?"

"Maybe. And the 'eternal city' is obviously Rome. 'Emperor's sister'; well, there were quite a few emperors whose family members were buried in Rome. But how many women had the authority to build their own tombs elsewhere? But maybe she did it without authority, and that's why she wasn't buried there." Lo huffed. "This is hopeless without more context."

"Hang on. What about Rome? I thought that was the capital city or something, right, so maybe we should look in Rome for the next clue?" Edward tried weakly to help.

"Rome is massive; just being there wouldn't make a difference at all, unless we knew where to start. And it wasn't always the capital city. Constantinople, or Istanbul, as it's known today, was once the capital. And not to mention, 'Rome' was divided into eastern and western empires by Diocletian," Lo's voice trailed off. Capital city. The term was used often enough today, but Roman's had another word for it—*Caput*. Literally, head. The head of the body or, in some cases, the head of the state. If caput in this context meant capital city, then they were looking not for Rome but for a different city with an empty tomb built by an emperor's sister which had three empty coffins in it. And if this woman, whoever she was, built a tomb in the capital of the Roman Empire, she would have made the building special, perhaps in the shape of a cross. Christianity had spread through the empire not long after Christ himself had lived. "I've just remembered. Constantinople was named so by Constantine."

"That makes sense." Ed nodded.

"But it was Theodosius who is considered the last ruling emperor of both Eastern and Western Rome."

"Nope, you lost me. Thought we said Rome was already split by the Dioclete guy." Ed went back to sipping his smoothie.

"It was divided but not officially split with different emperors until…" Lo paused and smiled, seeing Edward's face scrunched up in an attempt to understand. "It's complicated. But the bottom line is Theodosius had children, one of which became emperor of the Western Roman Empire. And that emperor had a sister who convinced him to move the capital city."

"See!" Edward's excitement made Jane jump. "I told you we should go to Rome!"

"She didn't move the capital to Rome. She moved it to a small port city in Northern Italy." Lo was too busy typing into her phone to notice Jane make a face at Edward's incorrect statement. "Ravenna. Galla Placidia was the sister of Emperor Honorius; she moved the capital to Ravenna and had a church complex built there. The church is destroyed, but the mausoleum remains...in the shape of a cross."

"How are you so smart?" Edward asked.

"I'm not. I used Google." Lo waved her phone in his face triumphantly.

"Looks like we're going to Italy." Jane leaned back in her chair.

Harlow picked up her smoothie, finally feeling interested enough to drink it. "Look, you two...you don't have to come."

"Do you think I just sat through this history lesson to not join in the fun?" Jane snapped. "I'm your friend, Lo. Of course I'll go. I don't really understand why or what exactly we're after, but I'll go."

"This quest or whatever bullshit we want to call it, it's mine, not yours. And I know both of you are skilled enough to lay low until all this blows over. Although, Edward, I have a feeling you might have to forfeit your battle with the homeowners association."

"Not a chance. I'll be joining you to save the world like Indiana Fucking Jones. And then the homeowners association will be offering to build my gazebo for me. You know you had me from the second you set foot through my kitchen window." Edward smiled.

Lo shook her head and felt more confident than she had in the past few days. Edward's yeses meant more than

Jane's, although she would never admit it out loud and felt bad for even thinking it.

Chapter Sixteen

Margo paced back and forth, praying they would find the answer soon. Leon and Sam were bent over what they had managed to copy at the bank. They had no clue as to what the pictures might mean. Perhaps it was a cypher of sorts.

The redhead took a shaky breath in. Her gran had told her stories of Jesus and God, stories about being fishers of men, and here it was in front of her. An odd picture of just that.

Of course, how could she be so blind? She snatched a Bible out of the drawer in the nightstand. *God bless the Gideons*, she thought. Hotel rooms would be odd without one of these stocked in their drawers. But maybe it isn't about the Bible at all?

"Sam, how good is your Latin?" Margo asked.

Yes, Margo was nothing if not determined. Gran had given the cancer to her daughter, Margo's mother; bad genetics was what the doctors called it. And, now, her little niece, not yet 12, was sick with the same bone cancer. This time, it wasn't going to win; she would find whatever she needed to and get the money promised to her.

Her phone rang that day, and she almost hadn't answered it. Luckily, she had. Who would have thought a silly professor's live interview would spark such controversy? This would be easy money; academics were a brainless bunch after all. All she'd have to do was send a few bullets flying, follow some old paper trail, and she'd have her money.

Sometimes cancer needed cold hard cash for research and treatment in order to be beaten.

No matter what happened, Margo was finding Eden.

Chapter Seventeen

Seven years ago.

It took Harlow a week to wrap her head around the existence of Eden, but when she arrived at the conclusion the professor was telling the truth, she was fully onboard to help him with whatever he needed. Tiproil's plan was coming to fruition; Harlow was the one he had been searching for. She was going to help him, in more ways than one.

It was still snowing outside, but the New Year had passed. A new semester on campus meant a renewal of energy for everyone. Tiproil was excited to meet with Harlow today, and when she showed up in his office, he couldn't keep the smile off his face. She was such a special girl, and she had no idea what was in store.

"It began years ago in Europe. I was working on a new research paper and stumbled upon some work that had been all but forgotten in the archives of the public library. A man named Giovanni had this unpublished dissertation of sorts; a theory on Eden being real. He had made it his mission to hunt down information on it back in the 1700s.

"I began to read it, and the more I read, the more I connected the dots to what I already knew. I spent the rest of my time there digging and came up with the truth. The Garden of Eden is real, and there are some people in this world who know about it. Giovanni recorded a series of coded papers in the 1700s with all the information he found on the Garden, including a series of codes from a clue composed back in 1000 A.D."

"So, you found some old papers that talked about an even older paper and that let you know Eden was real?" Harlow was skeptical about this, and rightfully so.

"The original paper Giovanni found was composed around 1000 A.D. No one knows who the author was; most likely a monk or someone in some holy order who stumbled upon the clues to Eden. Of course, being 700 years old during Giovanni's time, the vellum they were written on was decaying." Tiproil turned the papers to a quote scrawled in ink.

'Be it God's will to destroy the instructions; they should not entirely be gone from the earth. I leave my notes in God's hands, trusting that whoever finds them will know what to do with them.'

"Giovanni made specific notes that were encoded. He hid them for safekeeping and destroyed the original."

"So, someone around 1000 A.D. wrote down the last set of clues on how to find Eden, and several hundred years later, Giovanni discovers them and sees that they're falling apart. He decides to copy them down, encode them, and hide them?"

"Yes."

"And you stumbled upon his notes about this?"

"Yes."

"And then you went and found Giovanni's papers?"

"Yes."

"And where were his notes hidden?"

"He meant, literally, 'God's hands.' I had to break open a statue of Christ at the Louvre, and hidden in his hands were the papers. Needless to say, the Louvre will never ask me back for another research grant."

"Okay." Harlow felt her brain was finally understanding everything. "Why not follow them and find the Garden yourself? Why did Giovanni hide the papers instead of finding Eden?"

"He did not want to find the Garden. Only protect it."

"Where are the coded papers now?" Harlow felt her heart rate quicken.

"Locked away." Tiproil motioned to a key. "I have a safety-deposit box in the city. I figure, for now, that's the safest place, but the problem isn't the papers themselves; it's the copies of the papers."

"Copies?"

"Giovanni made several copies of not only his notes on Eden but the original clue he found on the paper from 1000 A.D. I've tracked down six, the only six in the world, I believe." They sat in silence for a moment as the snow fell outside the university.

"The British Museum has an extensive storage facility. Harlow, hypothetically speaking, if I needed something... well, if I needed something that someone else owns, do you know of anyone who could get it for me?" He handed her the bottle of black-label whiskey he kept hidden with the file of papers on Eden in his bottom cupboard. His dark eyes watched her steadily as she took a sip.

"Are you saying you want me to steal something?" Harlow didn't try to hide her smile.

"Not steal." Tiproil's eyebrows came together as he thought. "Reallocate."

"What exactly needs reallocated? I may know someone who can help." Harlow was finally understanding why he had selected her. While most of the professors steered clear, Tiproil had befriended her. More importantly, he had shown her his work.

"These six papers have accidentally fallen into the collections of various institutions, and it has come to my attention that we need them."

Chapter Eighteen

It was a humid day in April, much different from the weather the trio had left from back in the States. The sun was just beginning to dip below the trees; the flight had taken all the daylight, but, mercifully, it was only a ten-hour trip with no layovers. Harlow wasn't sure how her companions would have survived if it had been any longer. Edward threw up twice, once because of turbulence, and the second time because he looked at his own vomit. Jane typically had an iron stomach, until the scent of Edward's vomit permeated into her row of seats.

A weary-eyed retired thief and a red-eyed assassin stood on the curb with no interest in sightseeing or helping their friend locate the Mausoleum of Galla Placidia. It was at least a two-hour drive from where they had landed in Venice.

"We should be able to take a taxi straight to the mausoleum, but I want to give them the name of a cafe or something close to it so no one suspects anything." Harlow had managed to get several hours of sleep on the flight and was ready to find the next clue and move on. While Edward's vomit hadn't caused her stomach to become upset, her dream of Tiproil being shot repeatedly caused it to churn. She had done her best since the discovery of his death to ignore any and all thoughts of him, but she couldn't deny how it had shaken her to her very core.

Once outside on the streets, it took Harlow only a few tries to convince a driver to take them all the way to Ravenna. A short, tanned man with graying hair and a beard to match finally shook his head yes. He spoke little to no English, so the taxi ride was silent except for Harlow's effort to part mime part hand-signal to him. Eventually, he understood how they needed to stop so she could get Euros to pay him.

Harlow refused to sleep like her companions. She knew no Italian except for *Ciao*, but it was more than Edward's (his long-standing joke was pretending words such as *pizza*, *tortellini*, *spaghetti* were authentic). Fortunately, for everyone in the taxi, he was too tired and too jetlagged to attempt his jokes.

"*Qui, qui.*" Here, here. The overweight taxi driver pointed rapidly to a cafe with a red awning. It appeared to be gearing up for the evening; waiters were moving tables around and bringing up various bottles of wine from a storeroom.

"*Grazie!*" Harlow counted out the correct number of Euros, stumbling over the unfamiliar bills and coins.

The taxi drove off with a '*prego*' being mumbled from the driver. Edward and Jane stood facing away from Lo and the empty spot the driver had just been. They were staring across the street, through a small grove of trees where a brick building sat inconsequentially. Four small, square rooms stuck out squatly from a slightly larger, square tower in the center. The tiled roof. It was so unimposing, Harlow looked up and down the street to find another building, certain it couldn't be that one.

"That's it?" Jane asked. "We flew ten hours, and I had to smell Ed's vomit for *this*?"

Edward shot her a dirty look, then noticed Harlow's uncertain look. His heart tugged in his chest; they hadn't helped her decode the first message, and she was worried she was wrong.

"Of course it's bland. They wouldn't want to attract attention to anything, right?"

"Right." Lo smiled softly. "And there's only one way for us to find out." They took off across the street as the last light from the sun faded. The humidity hung in the air but only slightly. Harlow knew it would get chilly before long.

"Front door, no guard, no cameras," Edward noted. "Isn't that odd for a historical sight?"

"Not in Italy." They worked on picking the locks together. "The whole damn country is basically a historical sight. You can't break ground here without uncovering some type of Roman city. They understand the importance of history, but there's a point where it can become a hindrance to progressiveness."

"Never thought I'd hear you say that."

"I'm full of surprises." The final lock clicked and the door was opened. Jane meandered beside them, and, together, the group opened the door to a cool, musty smell. The steps down were steep, and they had to go slowly. By the light of her flashlight, Jane found the light switch for a rudimentary set of construction lights strung throughout the small building. Various sizes of tarps hung across the ceiling and were draped across the floor; a small renovation project was being undertaken, but cloth covers did nothing to hide the breathtaking interior.

"Harlow, I definitely believe you've found the right building." Edward stood between the two women, just as stunned as them. Even with the dim lighting, the beauty of the mausoleum could not be hindered. Mosaics covered almost every surface, their tiny squares of glass and ceramics glinted, sparkled, and shone down on the three below.

Four alcoves tunneled out from the center of the small building, forming the shape of a cross. The barrel-vaulted ceilings were covered in an intricate; mosaic adorned it; white, silver, scarlet, and gold-patterned stars dotted what almost looked like a midnight-blue night sky. The pattern swirled around the ceiling, changing and moving in the light.

"How do we find the next clue?" Edward asked. He was the only one able to speak, but his questions broke both the women from the trance of the tomb.

"The poem in the papers—what did the translation say?" Lo didn't bother taking out the papers; she knew Edward would remember.

"The head with three empty tombs; she built her cross with gardens above," he began.

"The old capital city of Ravenna, three empty tombs..." Harlow walked around the small interior, pointing to three large rectangles sitting in each alcove. "Must be the three empty sarcophagi." She continued to walk, her pace quickening. She lifted several of the tarps only to find uninteresting content beneath. Panic began to set in once more. How long was it going to be until someone noticed the lights were on in here?

"Did you know this place made it onto the U.N.E.S.C.O. World Heritage List in 1996?" Jane's question reminded everyone she was still present.

"I did not, Jane. Thanks for that info." Harlow shook her head and continued her search.

"Her tomb she built, body not below; the eternal city for the emperor's sister."

"More lines explaining how she isn't buried here." Nothing. There was no sign of anything except an old and firmly tiled floor, looking very much how it should.

"Did you know the building is actually sinking? It used to be several feet taller from the outside, but the ground has risen after all these years," Jane's voice again echoed off the walls.

"The garden grows in the light for the woman seated in her throne," Edward finished the poem. Neither responded to Jane.

"In the 1500s, this place was set on fire. No one knows if it was on purpose or by accident."

"Jane, how on earth do you know this?" Both Edward and Harlow turned to see Jane holding a glossy brochure.

"You snagged that from the entrance when we were picking the lock, didn't you?" Edward asked.

"They're free for visitors!" she snapped back.

"Are we visitors if we break in?"

"What does your brochure say about the Garden of Eden or the downfall of mankind?" Harlow moved back into the center where her two friends stood, bickering.

"Nothing." Jane shrugged, turning from Edward. "But it does mention one of the mosaics being titled 'Garden of Eden.'"

Before Jane could move, Harlow had ripped the brochure from her hands. She pointed to the tiny, italic font written in poor English, blending in with the background colors below a picture of the ceiling.

"The ceiling? The ceiling is called the Garden of Eden?" Harlow looked above her. *Gardens above.* The tiles she thought were stars could easily be flowers. Flowers swirling in a sea of vines and other plants. If this were true, if the ceiling itself was the Garden, then what did they have to do to get the next clue? Smash it all? She shuddered at the thought.

"It's supposed to grow in the light according to our cryptic poem. But there's light already shining." Edward scratched his head.

"There has to be more. Another hint, another something." Harlow was getting frustrated. She walked away from the group again, heading toward the far end where one differently shaped sarcophagus sat. Above it, in the double arches underneath the garden mosaics, were strange depictions. Two men stood in togas, arms outstretched, forming a type of frame around the slim window. Beneath them was an angel; he stood across from a dresser of sorts with the doors open and books sitting on the shelves within. Between the angel and his furniture was a grate with fire beneath it.

"I know what we have to do." Harlow spun around quickly to face Edward and Jane. "We need to set this place on fire."

Chapter Nineteen

"We are not setting anything on fire, let alone a small building we're inside, you pyromaniac!" Edward yelled. Of all the idiotic ideas Harlow had come up with in the time since they'd met, this might have been her most unintelligent one yet. An old, small building like this going up in flames with them inside would be suicide.

"Hear me out," Lo began.

"There's only one exit!" Jane screamed. "Why would you set a place on fire when there's only one exit?"

"Edward, say the last line," Harlow ordered, ignoring her friends' panic.

"The garden grows in the light for the woman seated in her throne." He paused. "It says nothing about a fire or us dying in that fire."

"Besides, the place is already lit up. With lights!" Jane's voice remained at a high, strained octave.

"No, these lights are fake. When the mausoleum was built, it would've been by torchlight, not L.E.D. bulbs."

"I think these are fluorescent actually," Edward corrected her.

"Either way." Lo shot him a dirty look. "We need legitimate light. Firelight."

"Why not sunlight? They had that back then, didn't they?" Jane spat.

"Do you want to wait around in here for eight more hours until the sun rises?" Harlow asked. She began to search her pockets for a lighter. She didn't smoke, but it was never a bad idea to keep one in hand should odd occasions like this arise. "Besides, I don't think sunlight would do the trick; otherwise loads of people who walked in here during the day would have been able to see where the next clue was."

"Good point." Jane nodded, suddenly completely onboard with the plan.

"Okay, I need everyone to empty their pockets and their backpacks for flammable materials. Any type of combustible, anything." Harlow clutched the small lighter while rooting through her bag, pulling out any insignificant material she could locate.

Edward and Jane began to do the same. The meager pile on the cold stone floor began to grow. Edward was unsure if this idea was a good one, let alone if it was going to work. Of course, the sanity in all of this was nonexistent, but there had to be some logic contained somewhere. Perhaps in the poem? There was no talk of where to place a bonfire inside the mausoleum. Was there a wrong place to put one?

"Why is it when you're in my life," he looked at Harlow, "weird things start to seem normal?"

Lo simply smiled and shrugged. Her jacket was falling down one shoulder, hair as messy and frizzy as can be, but despite all of this, she was gorgeous. Edward knew she could be covered in dirt from head to toe, and as long as she had the wild look in her eyes and the smile on her lips, he would find her irresistible.

Harlow bent down and slowly began to light the edges of the pile while Jane and Edward looked on. Edward snatched the brochure from Jane's hands and tossed it onto the growing flame. He simply shrugged. "It's flammable."

Jane stomped off toward the door to snag another brochure; he had no doubt. Edward chucked; at least he could still make himself laugh by annoying his least favorite assassin. The fire was fully ablaze now, but Harlow had disappeared on the other side. He could have sworn he saw her pull more items from her bag and toss them onto the pile.

"Harlow, be careful," his deep voice echoed off the walls. He looked up toward the ceiling where the Garden was supposed to be hiding but saw nothing.

"Something needs to be happening. Do you see anything happening?" Harlow was nervous; he could tell before she appeared next to him, zipping her book bag shut and tossing it over her shoulders. "What could we be missing?"

"Nothing, Harlow, just give it a moment." He reached his hand over to steady her. The fire was definitely growing now, outshining the construction lights. A large tarp fluttered in the disturbed air. He thought back over the poem. "Lo, what about the throne? We figured everything out except that part. Maybe that's where the garden is?"

"At least we're on the side by the exit." Jane reappeared through the growing smoke, holding two brochures in her hand, just like Edward had suspected. She bent her head back to gaze at the ceiling. "I don't see Eden."

"The garden grows in the light for the woman seated in her throne." Edward stood in between the two women, repeating the final line from the poem.

"For the woman seated in her throne," Harlow whispered.

Suddenly, the edge of a tarp blew loose from its meager holdings; before anyone knew what was happening, it had caught fire. The fire spread quickly, almost with inhuman speed, so that in an instant, the fire had tripled in size, threatening to consume the entire mausoleum.

"This is why you don't set things on fire!" Edward yelled. "We need to leave, now."

"No, we need to find the throne!" Jane snapped back. "Look at the ceiling!"

All three heads looked upward. In the intense heat given off from the flames, the mosaics began to swirl and morph. Even through the darkening fog, it was clear; the ceiling, the garden, appeared to be growing.

"I can't see what it's changing into!" Jane squinted through the smoke. The trio took a step closer to the door as the fire grew, still stronger.

"It grows for the woman seated in her throne," Harlow said softly at first. "We need to find the woman seated in her throne!" she all but shouted.

"So where's the throne?" Edward yelled. The flames threatened to overtake them; the smoke was beginning to burn their eyes.

Harlow closed her eyes, trying to remember what the mausoleum looked like before the fire and smoke and threat of imminent death. The three sarcophagi were the only significant pieces of furniture, and none of them were certainly a throne. Or were they? The one in the center had two, large, rectangular blocks on the sides, almost like arms on a chair.

It was now or never, because if she hesitated any longer, the flames would be blocking the way. She'd never be able to even see if her hunch was correct; the entire mausoleum would be burnt down. She would be letting Tiproil down.

Without another moment's thought, Harlow shoved her book bag into Jane's hands and leaped through the flames. Her black Chuck Taylors pushed her body up onto the sarcophagus below the odd mosaic, the throne meant for Galla Placidia. She sat on the warming stone and looked up at the ceiling.

It was then she could see it completely, the magic she had doubted all those months ago in the professor's office. It was thought magic could never be real in any capacity, but as the tiles above her heated, she realized what it meant to take something science could explain and simply describe it as divine.

The garden was growing, morphing, changing into a shimmering, glimmering wonderland, beckoning Harlow toward it. Without noticing what she was doing, Harlow's hand began to reach upward, slowly but steadily as if being pulled by a hypnotic force. The tiled ceiling had come alive, no longer a mosaic.

Harlow's hand had almost reached its destination before she understood what she had been drawn toward. One tile, almost directly above the throne, completely invisible from any other vantage point, was glowing brighter than the rest. No. Not brighter, differently. Instead of shimmering and glistening, this one had an incandescent glow about it, as if it were made from another material entirely that reacted differently to heat. Somewhere in the back of Harlow's mind, she registered that was probably exactly what it was. But here, now, all she knew was that her fingertips could just brush against the tile...

BANG.

The tile exploded like a canister that held too much pressure inside. The noise recoiled viciously around the stone walls, almost causing Harlow to lose her footing. She felt a sharp pain on the top of her head. Something had fallen from the small explosion. A tile perhaps? No, it had part of the tile on one side, but it was larger than that.

Harlow quickly scooped up the fallen artifact; it was hot in her hands, but she barely noticed. The tile was large in depth, not width. In fact, it wasn't a tile at all, it was a small box.

Chapter Twenty

It was dark outside, but the fierce fire burning inside the mausoleum gave off enough eerie light to make the scene visible to anyone not knocked unconscious by the vicious blast Harlow had accidentally set off.

Edward was not one of those people. He found himself somewhere in between awake and asleep, as if he'd been forced to close his eyes while underwater. Everything was muffled and dark, but he could hear sirens off in the distance and faint lights through shut eyelids. Brightness here, darkness there. None of it made any sense. He tried to focus his mind, but the darkness felt comforting, and he let himself slide deeper into it.

Sometime later, Edward felt his brain begin to surface; thoughts poked above the water level, making tiny ripples he couldn't quite understand. He thought they were in Europe. He thought they were inside an old crypt. He thought they had purposefully set fire to the room they were in.

The dampened noises began to grow more acute; he could hear coffee spitting through a machine. They *had* set fire to a mausoleum; Edward forced his eyes completely and cringed at the harshness of reality. He was lying in a bed, staring at a cracked, off-white hotel ceiling. A lone light bulb with a corroded silver fixture was screwed off center in the ceiling, but it was turned off.

Where exactly was he?

"Morning." It was Jane's voice he heard.

"Tell me the short version of what happened," Edward croaked through clenched teeth as he fought to sit upright. His whole body protested angrily. His eyes shut tightly in an attempt to keep some of the pain at bay. He had liked the dullness of before.

According to Jane, Harlow had leapt off the throne and through the fire to run out into the night, only to find Edward is on the ground, unconscious. She had pulled Edward far enough away from the crowd to avoid suspicion. Jane managed to find them, and the trio waited quietly until he was alert enough to stumble down the street and into a taxi who took them to a hotel.

"That explosion was nasty." Jane passed him a cup of coffee, black and steaming. "Whatever Harlow hit coupled with the chemicals catching on fire in that building, it sent me flying through the door halfway across the yard and you back into a wall where you blacked out."

"Where's Harlow?" Edward felt panic rise up in his chest.

"She's next door, working on deciphering the clue we found. Well, the clue *she* found."

"She's okay?" He knew it didn't matter what Jane said. The panic in him wouldn't dissipate completely until he saw her.

"Go look." It was as if she read his mind. She continued to speak slowly for his benefit while he poked his head through the open connecting door. "For some reason, the explosion didn't hit her. I've only seen that happen maybe twice accidentally. Normal explosions have a 360-degree radius, but this one didn't. The force seemed to shoot at us near the entrance and nowhere else."

Harlow's messy, brown hair frizzed out down her back, slightly damp from the shower she must've taken not too long ago. Edward could tell, even from behind, she was biting her lip and furrowing her eyebrows together at the puzzle in front of her. He knew she would want to remain uninterrupted as she thought.

"It isn't likely the place was booby trapped with a shape charge," Jane continued. She sat on the edge of the only bed in the room, intently focusing on her gun, waiting for Edward to return. "Harlow and I both thought through it; the Romans simply had no need to harm whoever was searching for Eden. Plus, none of the other clues were rigged before."

"So it was some freak, accidental explosions that almost killed you and me." Edward reluctantly let Harlow out of his sight and sat back in the bed.

"Yeah, it looks like it. The clue is inside some type of box. Give her another ten minutes or so, and we can go bug her to get a look at it." Jane set the gun on the floor and flipped upside down so her blonde hair was sprawled out on the floor and her sock-covered feet were uncomfortably close to Edward.

Moments passed in an unpleasant silence. Edward wanted to go back to sleep or at least feign unconsciousness so he didn't have to sit through the agonizing seconds Jane mindlessly flipped through Italian T.V. upside down.

Finally, she shut it off, and the room darkened slightly from the loss of light.

"You know, I was with her when they tested her I.Q." He could hear Jane scratching at the metal on her handgun. She was still hanging off the edge of the bed. "We were both taking some time off."

Edward remained silent. He never asked Harlow or Jane about this, but he knew they had spent time in an institution of sorts. It was how they met. Neither knew the other was part-time invested in felonious activities, but their friendship stuck.

"She would never admit it, but she was scared. They showed she was at 146."

"I'm assuming that's high?"

Jane snorted, but it quickly turned into a cough from her upside-down position. "Yeah. That's higher than Einstein's I.Q. which, in case you didn't know, is very high." She paused for a moment, her hands still running over her gun. "I would've thought yours is somewhere close to that, given—"

"No," Edward cut her off quickly. He was glad he couldn't see the look on her face. Suddenly, he realized his coffee didn't taste so good after all. "My I.Q. is nowhere near that, I'm sure. I have a gift, a talent if you will. I can remember things distinctly, but I don't have the brainpower to understand them. Or *forget* them, really."

They sat silently for a moment, listening to Harlow as she mumbled words neither understood. Jane lifted herself up onto the bed, shaking her head at the overabundance of blood finally draining from her skull.

"What use is remembering numbers if you can't do the math problem?" For the first time, Jane seemed to truly understand Edward's brain. Everyone who knew of his memory trick hailed him as some type of special, spectacular sideshow. They loved asking him odd questions in bars or during sports games, but that's where it ended.

Edward hated it—he was stuck with a bad memory, an inability to forget. There was nothing really special about it at all except information came in and never went out.

"I can read people the first few minutes I meet them, and I can remember the exact words they say, but I don't know what to do with the information. I can barely move on after a fight with anyone because their words always replay in my head." He took a deep breath, trying to steady himself. "Won a shit ton of money at poker in my lifetime. Hell, I used to make some mad money at all sorts of card games, but as far as intelligence goes, I'm no smarter than you."

"Hey, watch it." Jane smiled. "I'm not completely stupid."

"Oh, I know." Edward turned away. He wanted the conversation to end.

"Let's go check on our little Einstein." Jane stood up and unsteadily walked through the doorway to where Harlow was seated. She heard them instantly and turned around. The bright computer screen behind her showed several pictures of what appeared to be a very old church with a baptismal font.

"Have either of you been baptized?"

Chapter Twenty-One

Six years ago.

Harlow glanced up and down the hallway one last time before turning the lock pick and opening the door to the professor's office. Once inside, she gently laid down her most recent treasure: the sixth and final copy of Giovanni's. The handwritten card went on top; the finishing touch.

She turned to leave and ran right into Tiproil.

"Class let out early," was all he said. He was disguising how happy he was to see Harlow.

"I got back from Greece a day early," was all she said in return, trying to hide how thrilled she was to see him.

"You got the last one?"

"Easier than the other five. And thank you for the first-class ticket. It was way better than riding in coach."

"I figured I'd splurge for our last adventure."

"Last adventure?" Surely he didn't mean this was it?

"It's mostly bookwork for a while. I have all the papers I know of."

"You still want my help, right?" Harlow was worried he might say no.

Tiproil didn't answer right away. He removed his spring jacket and hung it on its hook, then slid past Harlow and sat down in his worn office chair. "I would be thrilled if you could help me work through some of this."

Harlow didn't know if he was telling the truth or not, but she didn't care. He hadn't said no, and that was all that mattered to her.

"Can I ask you what's really inside Eden? It's been bothering me for a while now. If it's just a garden, why not let people find it?"

"It's much more than 'just a garden.' There are different discussions about what the Garden of Eden holds inside. Different interpretations."

"But there's only one story of the Garden of Eden in the Bible." Harlow wanted to argue with him. Maybe if she got him wound up, she would find out what was wrong, but he didn't take the bait.

"Yes, but as we discussed, there are many different versions of the Bible, all of which have a slightly different flavor to them."

"Okay. So Adam and Eve are told not to eat the apple, and they do because a serpent tells them to."

"Firstly, you know it isn't an apple. The Bible never refers to a specific fruit, only that it grew on a tree. We can assume it was either a pomegranate or olive; both are known to have been grown in that region. Or it's possible it could have been something else entirely. But not an apple.

"Secondly, the danger comes from the tree the fruit is picked from. There are two forbidden trees, depending on the version of the Bible you read."

"The Tree of Knowledge of Good and Evil, and the Tree of Life."

"I'm impressed." Tiproil shifted in his chair. He was happy he had chosen Harlow, even if she had a short, illogical temper.

"Do you think it really is forbidden by God? Maybe it's like Indiana Jones and the Ark of the Covenant when the Nazi's faces melt off."

"Let's be realistic here, Harlow." Tiproil hid a smirk. "Do you really think a fruit has magical powers? Most likely not. Truth is often stranger than fiction; if you want my academic, educational guess, I would say the fruit reacts with the human body in some unknown way. Perhaps it acts like heroine or some type of crazy drug that causes the person to lose their mind." The professor took a deep breath. "What I fear it might be, is a biological weapon of sorts. Eve ate the apple and went crazy, so they left Eden forever and went to great lengths to keep Eden hidden forever."

"Whatever it is, it's powerful."

"Whatever it is, we must never find out."

"I know." Harlow nodded as she reached for the old Bible they kept nearby. She flipped through it and read the passage from Genesis, "Whatever is in there, no one can ever find out."

Chapter Twenty-Two

They left the hotel before the sun broke through the clouds. Coincidentally, it was also before the concierge was up at the front desk, ready with their room bill. The bruised and battered trio headed to the train station with few words being passed between them. Edward had stopped asking questions to Harlow; all he knew was they needed to go to the Baptistery of Florence, which was also called the Baptistery of St. John's, which was somehow related to the clue she had found in the ceiling of the mausoleum.

He watched the city and countryside speed by through the window of the almost-deserted train. Harlow sat in the worn seat next to him, Jane across a small space for their legs and luggage. Neither spoke. It would take less than two hours to get to Florence.

Harlow nervously rolled the box around in her hands. It was small with blue, black, and white tiles checkered on all six sides, no bigger than Edward's hand. It seemed to him that Harlow never stopped fidgeting with it. She noticed early on some of the tiles were loose, but no matter what she tried, she could not get it to open.

The box was wrapped in vellum, ancient and cracked, containing a few words.

Baptized above Mars.
Garden in the East.
Sunlight shows the Key.

"It's less poetic than the last one," Edward pointed out.

"Maybe they realized how idiotic this all is," Jane mumbled.

Harlow ignored them both. "The Baptistery of Florence was built overtop a temple dedicated to Mars, the Roman god of war. The Cathedral Santa Maria del Fiore is across the plaza; that's a major tourist attraction, so we have to be careful.

"The baptistery is less ornate on the outside except for the doors. Four sets of massive doors with gold inlay and sculptures decorate it. Originally, all of them faced east. Michelangelo called one set 'the gates of Paradise' because they depicted Eden. It makes sense this is where the next clue is."

"Way easier than the last one. Maybe they did change their minds." Edward leaned back in his seat. Something was bothering him, but he couldn't figure it out. A lot had happened in the past 48 hours, including a bank heist gone wrong, the accidental murder of unknown baddies who were possibly still chasing them, and the loss of his gazebo.

Baptized above Mars. Garden in the East. Sunlight shows the Key. The words flashed through Edward's mind. Why was the first clue so ornate and this one so simple? Were there no other temples or buildings dealing with Mars that might fit the only reference to where the next location was? Then there were the papers he and Harlow had stolen from the bank. Why all that fuss over one clue? If they'd beaten the baddies to the first clue, there was no trail left to follow. Why go after the next clue? Most importantly, what was in the damned box he'd almost gotten blown up for?

"Harlow, I think we should talk." Edward looked over at his friend who was fast asleep in the dim light. He couldn't bring himself to wake her. He felt a sudden wave wash over him as he looked at her, not because of how peaceful she looked, but because he pretended, if only for a few moments, things hadn't fallen apart in the way they had.

They had finished a heist in Mexico, pulled it off perfectly. The only unplanned part was Harlow's surprise visit to his old apartment. He could still see her face, bright and happy, barely able to be seen over the box filled with his things he'd forgotten to pack up. Had he known she was coming, he would have told her not to, would have insisted on meeting her somewhere, would have told his wife not to come over.

But Harlow was there, standing in his doorway, stretching to stare over the overflowing box at Morgan, his estranged wife who had opened the door when Harlow knocked.

"Morgan, you know my business associate." He pushed by his wife in the doorway, trying to block her view of Harlow as if separating the two physically would keep them apart.

But it was too late; the damage had been done.

"You should've told me you were coming." The door closed, and Edward was standing out in the hallway with Harlow, the large box suddenly shoved in his arms.

"Take these," Harlow said nothing else and turned to leave.

"Lo, please, give me a minute to try and talk about—"
He struggled with the large box in his hands, almost
tumbling down the hallway after Harlow.

"You don't want to talk about it. You never do. Not
even when we have the opportunities to." She wasn't
running, wasn't walking away even. She turned to face
Edward, an odd calmness settling over her entire being. "I
understand, Ed."

"I can barely talk about it to myself let alone anyone
else." He wanted her to be mad, to yell and scream, to throw
a fit, but she stood there like stone while he began to break
down.

"Don't talk about it then. Let it be what it is." Harlow
took a step backward. "You married her before me. You
loved her before me."

"Lo..." Edward was crying now.

"You love her. I understand now. I was just..." She
shrugged. "I was something that happened in between
forever." Numbness spread throughout her entire body. "Go
be with your wife."

They were the last words she had said to him. He stood
in the hallway only a minute longer before collapsing to the
floor in tears. He had gone back inside with the box of junk
and tried to face his wife, tried to explain Harlow and his
tears. In the end, he settled for an easy lie: an affair that was
over as quickly as it had begun. She could learn to move on
if he could; of course, Edward never forgave himself for that
day.

Harlow had loved him truly, and he knew, even now,
she still did. But love and hate are so close. He knew Harlow
hated him only half as much as he hated himself.

Chapter Twenty-Three

Edward was glad it was dark outside when they got off the train. It was still too early for there to be many tourists around, the exception being those overly committed in seeing Italy at all odd hours of the day. He hadn't been to Europe often, but Edward was sure the city at 4 a.m. was no more a magical place than a city in the U.S. at the same time.

"The Cathedral Santa Maria del Fiore." Edward nodded toward the structure. Among a sea of terracotta-brown roofing and white siding, there jutted a massive structure. A wide plaza sprawled before it as if the city itself had moved aside to allow for the building's magnificence.

"Well, it's certainly easy enough to spot." Jane looked around her as if expecting someone to pop up and make a run for the cathedral before them. It was easy to find in the growing light. In truth, it would have been easy to find in the dark as well.

"Not so easy to pronounce." Harlow smiled at Edward's correct pronunciation.

"Am I correct in assuming *that*," Edward pointed toward a cylindrical building attached to the cathedral, smiling, "is the baptistery?"

"No. The one with the red roof is actually called the Domus." Harlow heard both Jane and Edward snicker. "It's not funny. It's actually quite interesting; it was constructed without using scaffolding because of the angle at which—" she stopped, knowing she'd lost the two of them to the word 'dome.'

"Over here is the Eastern Door; also known as the Gates of Paradise." Harlow ignored the continual chuckles from her comrades and walked briskly toward the baptistery. She had to crane her neck back to see the tops of the Eastern Door.

"There's the Genesis story." Harlow pointed to a panel. "You can see the angels casting Adam and Eve out of the Garden. There's the Tree, and it looks like they made that arch to represent the actual doorway to Eden."

Hand-carved relief scenes covered the double doors in ten, massive, rectangular panels running upward, five on each door. They were made out of what looked like gold, glistening as the early sun just began to poke through.

"Maybe we should just Google 'massive arches with angels floating around' and see what pops up?" Jane smirked.

"Maybe we should just break in and steal whatever we need to?" Harlow snapped as Jane failed to conceal another laugh. "The only entrance is through the North Gate now." She dropped her head away from the gates and walked around the circular baptistery to an official-looking area with small museum signs left out from the day before.

The North Gate was decorated similarly to the East Gate, except the golden scenes and figures were coming out of wood-carved squares. There were 28 squares divided into four columns of seven in each, lining these doors; an impressive sight, but definitely not the Gates of Paradise.

It was almost too easy to slip through the doors; they were closed but barely locked.

Edward took less than six minutes to unlock it. Not bad for coming out of retirement.

The inside of the baptistery was less impressive than the mausoleum; Edward noted that the outside of the mausoleum definitely looked less impressive than the baptistery. Dimly lit, the octagonal shape was discerning. A large, domed ceiling drew the gaze off all three criminals upward.

Drenched with gold, rows upon rows of mosaics shone, telling a circular story. Angels, saints, and Christ himself shone down on those who entered. Edward felt a chill slither up his spine; it was as if the holiness of this place was seeping into his bones.

He thought for a moment about the sparsity of the clue: *Garden in the East. Sunlight shows the Key.* The scene above was definitely shining like the sun. Maybe it would shine directly onto one of the eight walls where a key was hidden.

"What exactly are we looking for?" Edward asked. All three criminals began to wander around aimlessly, searching for anything that could possibly point them in the right direction. Statues with plaques in both English and Italian explanations were strategically placed around the octagon. Massive pillars with more sculptures dotted the outer walls. A shallow alcove with an altar was across from where the trio was standing.

"I'm not entirely sure," Harlow's voice was soft as she wandered further away from Edward, heading toward a strange, rectangular box pushed against a wall.

"Maybe there's a clue somewhere on this?" Edward pointed at a carved pedestal with a large basin atop it. Two small steps led up to it and a decorative gate surrounded it.

"That's the baptismal font," Harlow answered. She barely turned around, so focused on the massive stone box almost within her reach.

"What is that, Lo?" Edward walked toward her.

"A Roman sarcophagus," the words came out as a whisper. Harlow was fascinated.

"A coffin inside a baptistery. Nice." Edward cringed. He noticed the deeply carved figures on the outside of the marble sarcophagus appeared to be hunting a boar. "What is this doing in here?"

"This place was built on a Roman temple. And there's more than just one dead person in here." She pointed across the octagon to a sculpture seated between two pillars. "The Funeral Monument to the Anti-Pope, Pope John XXIII."

"Don't laugh, but... What's an anti-pope?"

Half a loving grin spread across Harlow's face. "The Church split in 1378 when two different men claimed to be the pope. They both had substantial backing by various countries and powerful entities; they even excommunicated each other."

"The more time I spend with you, the more confused I get about history." Edward shook his head. The two looked at each other for a moment, forgetting where they were. Edward felt an overwhelming compulsion to wrap his arms around Harlow and never let her go.

"What about the eastern door from earlier?" Jane's voice echoed into their ears, causing them to be brought to the present. The blonde was on the opposite section of the octagon, rummaging around in the dim light, looking for something. "If they were literally called 'Gates of Paradise' or whatever, maybe the clue is hidden in there."

"They could be. But I can't see the clue being hidden on the outside of the baptistery."

Harlow moved away from Edward to continue her search. "Of course, it did cross my mind the Gates of Paradise might hold the next clue..."

"Let's see what the Official Italian Tour Guides have written down here for us." Jane flapped open an informational brochure. Edward chuckled when she lit an offertory candle to use the flickering light to read.

"Very resourceful, Jane," Edward praised her. He had to give the assassin credit; she did have some creative ideas.

"Maybe we need to wait until sunlight to see what we need to see," Harlow mumbled.

She looked back up at the arched ceiling.

"Jane!" Suddenly, her head snapped back down. She sprinted across the floor to where Jane was standing, her quick hands tried to snatch the brochure away. "Why do you have this?"

"I need to be entertained somehow!" Jane managed to outmaneuver Harlow, forcing her body weight between them.

It was then Edward heard a soft rustling noise coming from outside. Perhaps the plaza was coming to life with early-rising tourists and natives.

"You don't even like to read this stuff," Harlow snapped, nearly out of breath from the scuffle.

"Harlow, I want to talk about the clues, about Eden." Edward wanted them to stop before they hurt each other. He wanted to know what that weird noise was. He wanted to know what they were looking for exactly. In short, he wanted answers.

"Give it here!" Harlow was nearly yelling at the top of her lungs. Edward began to move over toward the girls. He had never seen Lo get upset over someone attempting to educate themselves. The rustling noise was growing louder. Perhaps it wasn't tourists or natives after all.

But what else could it be?

"Harlow!" Edward raised his voice to snap her out of her trance. Someone was going to hear her; the entire town was waking up.

Harlow ignored Edward, her chest rising up and down searching for air, her hand limp by her side like a snake debating when it wants to strike again.

What is wrong with her? he thought.

"It says here the actual doors were moved to the Opera del Dumo Museum..." Jane read rapidly, afraid Harlow would snatch the pamphlet way at any moment. "Why did you bring us here if—?"

It was in that moment Edward realized what the noise was—not people outside in the plaza but people attempting to come *inside* the baptistery. He began to yell for the girls to run, his voice clashing into Jane's.

Three loud bangs nearly burst the eardrums of every person inside the baptistery. Edward stumbled over to where Harlow and Jane stood, hands over his screaming ears. He saw both girls hidden behind pews, their guns drawn. His eyes methodically scanned for some sign or hint of which gun had gone off, but he knew he must be reading the scene incorrectly. Harlow would never fire her gun inside, would she?

Chapter Twenty-Four

"We need another way out!" Jane voiced the obvious. They had completely forgotten about the fight over the museum brochure, but Edward saw her stuff it quickly into her pocket.

"Another way out? This is a place for babies to get baptized, not a theme park with clearly marked emergency exits!" Harlow quipped.

"Those gunshots sounded like they came from inside. Let's move!" Edward's voice was strained. He grabbed both girls by their arms and sprinted, awkwardly, toward the only exit. They burst through into the bright light of dawn, startling pigeons and people who had been admiring the baptistery.

Edward looked around in an attempt to see who had fired the shots. Standing starkly out from the crowd of tourists in the plaza were three menacing shapes.

Harlow recognized their faces even from a distance; the same ones who had appeared in the bank and destroyed Edward's gazebo. "The Germans."

"I don't think they're here for the history," Jane mumbled. She adjusted the grip on her gun.

Edward once more yanked the arms of the girls, and all three took off, sprinting across the plaza toward the menacingly large Cathedral Santa Maria del Fiore. He turned his head to see the three Germans following suit.

The trio dashed through the open doors of the cathedral alongside tourists meandering in the early morning. If they weren't being chased by foreigners with guns who wanted them dead, they all might have been inclined to gasp at the view. The massively vaulted ceilings felt five times higher than the baptistery's. There were several hundred tourists inside, but the magnitude of space could have allowed for 500 more before feelings of crowdedness would even begin to take place.

Massive pillars arched upward to a vaulted ceiling decorated intricately with mosaics. A marble floor felt the click and clack of the trios rapid footsteps as they each rushed to find some type of hiding spot.

"Here!" Harlow yelled, motioning to a side channel inside the massive cathedral. They diverted from the main section and found they could pause for a moment and catch their breaths.

Screams came from the innocent tourists as they saw the fearsome Germans with guns burst into the peaceful cathedral. Shouts were heard, and a gunshot rang through the peaceful church.

"Maybe they've moved on from destroying gazebos to national landmarks," Edward said angrily.

"Would you give it up on the gazebo already!?" Jane snapped. "Harlow, where are we going?" She turned to look at her friend who was busy crouching down on the floor.

"This way." She slid her body around a sculpture. Jane and Edward followed with puzzled looks as Harlow's body had simply vanished, and there was no way the space behind the statue had enough room for three grown felons to hide. But since they didn't have much time to argue, seeing as they were about to be discovered any second, they slipped behind the sculpture to find a small doorway.

"Oh no. It's too cliché. We're going down into the crypt?" Jane swallowed nervously.

"Don't tell me you're nervous of some dead people?" Edward chuckled in the dark doorway. There was no way the Germans could see them; for a moment, he felt safe.

"We're not going down, we're going up." Harlow walked as fast as she could in the dim light down the crudely cut stone corridor, Edward and Jane stumbling behind her. "These passages were used by the builders. They'll wind over to Brunelleschi's Cupola and up to the top. I figure, if we make it all the way there, the Germans won't follow us."

"We sure they're German?" Jane asked, tripping over a stone and nearly crashing into Harlow.

"What is a cupola?" Edward ignored Jane's question. He couldn't care less what the baddies were called. "The Germans are chasing and trying to murder us. Who cares if we call them the wrong name?"

"Maybe they won't want to kill us if we get their nationality right!" Jane piped up. "And I think a cupola is—"

"Would you two focus please?" Harlow was a decent distance ahead, annoyed she had to stop and wait for them to catch up. "We don't discuss technicalities when there are gunmen involved. LET'S GO!"

Harlow knew tourists would kill for this kind of behind-the-scenes access to one of the most famous sites in Italy. They began to climb coarse steps, their uneven sizes making it challenging, and the threat of the Germans added terror to the mix. She was unable to feel even the slightest inkling of enjoyment.

"They're coming!" Edward's voice startled the girls. "I hear them."

The trio quickened their pace, almost sprinting. Suddenly, Jane stumbled over a particularly rocky step and a sickening thud reverberated around her body as her face smashed into a stone step several feet in front of her. The force of the fall caused her head to recoil backward like an unnatural bouncy ball; immediately Harlow and Edward could see a pool of blood leaking from her skull.

"Jane!" Harlow dashed back down the steps. Edward felt fear grip his heart. They couldn't stay and risk running into the Germans, and they certainly didn't have the strength to carry Jane, especially not with a severe head wound.

"Mmmm," Jane couldn't speak, but she wasn't completely unconscious. She picked her head up, blood flowing everywhere, and strained to open one eye to look at Harlow.

"Jane, hold on, okay? We're going to carry you to the top. There's a spot we can hide not too far up. Just hold on." Harlow bent to wrap Jane's arm around her shoulder, ignorant of her brown hair dipping in Jane's blood. It left a wispy trail behind as it dragged across the stone.

"Harlow," Edward searched for the right words. Touching her arm gently, he hoped she would understand they needed to leave Jane behind.

"Mmmm," Jane tried again to speak. It was clearly painful to move; Harlow was only making it worse. "MMMMM!" She was almost screaming now.

"Edward, help me!" Harlow yelled. Her blood-soaked hair was dripping down her back, staining her t-shirt.

"Mm-move!" Jane finally spoke the word that had been held captive. "Move! Go!" she could only speak one word at a time, and painfully so, but the message was clear:

Harlow and Edward were supposed to keep moving and leave her behind.

Chapter Twenty-Five

Margo hated running. Lord knew this job required too much of it. It was time for things to really start moving along; the plan had been thrown off long enough. Damn cardio and damn the Garden of Eden. Ever since the professor had revealed his clues the whole world seemed to lose their damn minds.

She sprinted up the stairs after Jane, Harlow, and Edward. Margo was glad she destroyed Edward's house and his gazebo out back, too. She was sick of chasing after them and she was especially pissed at what happened at the bank. Poor Leon was dead; the worst part was calling his wife and attempting to explain the situation. To make matters worse she'd had to spend hours dodging the police.

Never before had she wanted to put a bullet inside someone's skull more so than she did now.

She could hear their footsteps climbing upward on the stone steps. It would be impossible for them to get away; what goes up must come down.

They rounded the corner and that's when she saw her: Jane, lying unconscious, soaked in blood.

"Dammit!" This was not how things were supposed to happen. Jane wasn't the one who's skull she wanted to see smashed open. Panic surged through her body, her heart racing quicker than she'd ever thought possible. Adrenaline surged through every part of her body. What were they going to do with Jane? They needed the others, too.

"Find them!" Margo screamed at Sam and Georg. It was then Margo realized, sitting next to Jane, soaked in blood, that she just wanted to go back home.

Georg and Sam were careful to avoid the blood as they stepped around Jane and ran upward after Lo and Edward. Margo stayed behind, alone with Jane.

"Please, please don't die," she pleaded quietly with Jane's unconscious body. Her words spoken in Africans, were quiet. "You can't die on me. This whole fight will be useless if you die."

Georg and Sam were, as henchmen often are, not particularly detail oriented. They did as they were told and ran after Harlow and Edward. They chased them up the stone steps, but failed to notice a slenderly cut closet hidden in the stone facade which Harlow had tugged Edward into only moments before. The two prey hid, holding their breath in the darkness until their predators passed.

They would have to keep following the duo. All they could do was keep Jane alive, see what she knew, and hope the two thieves showed up on their radar at some point.

Chapter Twenty-Six

Five-and-a-half years ago.

"I don't get why I have to write all of these down," Harlow complained, her hand cramping. "And what is a 'celestial hierarchy' anyway?" It was the first decent spring day they'd had all year, and she wanted nothing more than to be outside in the sunshine. Instead, she had spent the past hour working with Tiproil on decoding the order of heavenly beings, their latest hunch in uncovering Eden.

"Stop complaining. Now, first comes."

"Angels, then archangels, principalities, powers, virtues, dominions, thrones, cherubim, and seraphim," she recited her writings like the good student she was not. "Why pray to angels when seraphim are the highest up?"

"Why are there so many types of cars on the road?"

"Because even a Honda gets the job done?" Harlow shrugged, concealing a smile. Tiproil had just compared a holy hierarchy to car manufacturers. "So, the authors of the bible specifically state cherubim guard the entrance in the east with swords on fire."

"No, just one cherubim. And east might be a technical term. Why do you think it turns in all directions?"

"Can you have a cardinal direction if there is no point of reference?"

"Exactly. But I believe the cherubim IS the point of reference. Find the cherubim, you find the entrance."

"Well, a large, naked baby with wings isn't exactly how I imagine God would hide the Garden of Eden."

Tiproil laughed from his stomach through his shoulders, the kind of laugh that you know is genuine and good. "No, no, he wouldn't hide it quite like that. Let's look into cherubim."

It didn't take more than an hour or so for Harlow to find what they had been looking for. There were what seemed like hundreds of references to cherubs in the Bible and outside of it. It turns out the true form of cherubim was a constant argument among the intellectuals. Not surprisingly, cherubs were viewed as winged babies, references to 'childlike faces' being the source for that depiction, but there was another school of thought having to deal with their role as protectors. In several other books of the Bible, they are discussed as protecting someone or something, and if this were the case for the Garden of Eden, a large baby with a flaming sword certainly wouldn't be appropriate.

"Heavenly beasts and divine guards. Beat that." Harlow tossed a book down atop the one Tiproil was reading. On it showed a large man-lion-winged hybrid guarding a dilapidated palace in what looked like Assyria or Persia.

"I had forgotten about the Lamassu Guards," Tiproil admitted with a smile. "Some type of animal hybrid with wings; that would certainly do the trick. Would scare off anyone, really."

"How terrifying would a pissed-off lion with wings and a flaming sword be?" Harlow smiled.

"You know, this is one of those times when the student has outdone the teacher." Tiproil leaned back in his chair. "I think you know just about all there is to know."

Harlow was taken aback. Was he dismissing her? "Except one thing." She closed the book on her lap. "What does the first clue say?"

"We aren't discussing that. You know not to read the papers you stole, and you know I can't tell you."

Chapter Twenty-Seven

Edward followed closely behind Harlow's every step, feeling relieved as the center-city noise grew fainter. The silence helped him think, helped him forget Jane's face fading away as they ran upward toward the light and she lay in her blood in the dimly lit stairway.

They continued to walk. Edward knew Harlow wanted to walk instead of catch a cab; walking helped her cope with leaving Jane behind. The Germans had her now—alive or dead, they didn't know. No gunshots had been heard, but how much care would they give Jane? If they took her as their captor, would they even bother keeping her healthy? Would they try to make contact? How in the hell would they manage that?

Edward didn't want to admit it, especially not to Harlow, but if Jane were his captive, she would be nothing but dead weight in her state. There was no purpose to keeping her alive or going to the lengths of getting medical assistance.

Harlow seemed to read his thoughts. He heard her cry silently into the night as she walked. Her pace slowed, her hand reached out and held onto Edward's, but she carried on in silence, only the occasional sniffle being heard. They walked up an empty road with a large hill emerging on their side, a brick wall built on top of it, hiding any trace of what might be concealed there. Edward could see treetops sticking out from the wall, but as they arrived at the ancient gate, he realized it was not a garden they were headed to.

Two, swirling, carved stones sat atop the gate, like angel wings with a sign in the center reading, in thick, black letters, 'CATACOMBE S. CALLISTO.'

"I should be concerned you're so familiar with how to get into the Roman catacombs," Edward spoke quietly so only Harlow could hear. There were a few tourists milling around the open area, debating if they should spend the Euros necessary to climb down and see the dead beneath the Eternal City at night.

"Not all Roman catacombs, just the San Callisto. Used to be my favorite place to sleep when I needed a nap." Harlow kept her hand in his and tightened her grip.

"Some days, I really think you need mental help."

"I know." She giggled slyly, forgetting for a moment about Jane. "But, for now, pretend you're Italian, okay?" She guided a silent and slightly concerned Edward toward the table by the entrance.

"*Ciao! Ciao!*"

Edward could barely understand the Italian Harlow spoke. He knew her knowledge was minimal, but the way she spoke with this tour guide, it didn't matter. They knew each other.

"*Il mio fidanzato.*" My boyfriend. She was introducing him as her boyfriend.

Edward tried to wipe the dumbstruck look off his face and replace it with a tender boyfriend type of gaze, but he knew from the furrowed brow appearing on the face of the aging tour guide he was out of practice.

"*Grazie!*" Harlow led Edward toward the entrance of the catacombs, still holding his hand tightly. She noticed how sweaty it was.

"You've got a lot of explaining to do," Edward mumbled.

"Bettina worked as a tour guide here since the day I first started breaking in. We've become friends over the years, or at least friendly toward each other. Italians want to see everyone paired off and happy with a partner, so when I told her I wanted to bring my new boyfriend to see the dead—"

"She was only too happy to oblige," Edward finished her sentence. "She wasn't—"

"Concerned about your age and mine?" Harlow finished his sentence this time. "Ed, they're Italian. You need to stop thinking like an American." She laughed and tugged him into the dark doorway.

They walked down into the earth, following an uneven floor filled with twists and turns. The further they went, the colder it felt. Edward shivered in the darkness, and the stale air was becoming unbearable.

"You spent a lot of time down here?" he asked skeptically.

"I love it. Just wait for the best part." Lo pushed on into the darkness, her flashlight shining the way.

The tunnel opened up into a wide, cavernous room. Harlow moved around quickly; she knew exactly where to go. Suddenly, the chamber was lit from a number of light bulbs placed strategically around. Edward wished the lights had remained off.

The walls were lined from the floor up to and including the ceiling with human skulls. Other various bones were interlaced to add a decorative touch; shinbones vertically outlined a pillar while pelvises marked an archway.

"Harlow, who are those people chasing us?" Edward tried to ignore the spooky feeling the catacombs were giving him.

"For the millionth time, Edward, I don't know who is after us. Why would I know them?" She was moving around, trying to find something.

"You were best friends with the professor who found Eden. Maybe he knew them."

"He didn't find Eden. He just found a real clue to Eden." She found what she was looking for and pulled a large plastic tub out from a dark corner. Inside it were sleeping bags, cash, and flashlights. "I hid this here a while back. Never know when you need a place to crash."

"Why on earth would you willingly choose this terrifying place?" Edward chanced a look around again, feeling the hairs rise on his neck.

"No one comes down here at night. It's safe. And it's directly under some buildings that have surprisingly strong Wi-Fi."

"I feel like Indiana Jones when they enter the catacombs in Venice."

"That movie is idiotic." Harlow shook her head. "Why would there be catacombs, an underground burial site, in a city built on stilts above water?"

"Well, when you put it like that…"

"Besides, no one is allowed to enter the catacombs under the Vatican without approval of the Vatican itself."

"Really?" Edward was curious. "What kind of riches do you think are down there?"

"None. Early Christians didn't bury things with their dead; they simply buried their bodies in elaborate patterns like this." She paused and her body tensed. "Edward, I should tell you—"

"You fired the shot inside the baptistery," Edward finished her thought with his suspicion. "So you either knew we were being followed or you just really wanted our cover to be blown."

"I had a hunch we were being followed."

Edward stood there for a moment, unsure of where to look or what to feel. He knew the thousands of skulls were watching him with their empty gazes, but they couldn't compare to the one Harlow was giving him. She held so much in her bright eyes—hope, fear, love, sorrow—how could he ever stay mad at her?

"And the baptistery...it wasn't...it wasn't a real clue. I made it up because of my hunch," Harlow's voice echoed off the dead. Their vacant stares and open jaws added to the immensity of her confession. All of her anger and frustration had fallen away like the flesh from the bones on the walls.

"You fired a gun inside a baptistery, got our cover blown, and, now, Jane is kidnapped because of a hunch?"

"It's better than a feeling." She shrugged meekly.

Not another word was said. The two began to arrange their sleeping bags, and Edward purposefully moved as close to Harlow as he could. Who cared what names she called him; this place was terrifying.

Edward had trouble sleeping, not to his surprise. He lay in the darkness on the cold floor with Harlow's body resting softly next to his. His eyes stared at the walls, knowing what was there even though he could not see it. There was more to the story and Harlow was holding back from him. He would talk to her in the morning. All he had to do was survive the night.

"Harlow, do you remember what Jane read from the pamphlet the other day?" It felt like a lifetime ago now. "There was a fire. Someone already tried to burn the mausoleum down." Edward's mind was beginning to hone in on the events that he had found particularly odd, replaying everything word for word.

"Back in the 1500s. I doubt they're still around, Edward."

"I just. I don't have a good feeling about this."

"We're following clues that are over a thousand years old to uncover the literal Garden of Eden. If you *did* have a good feeling, I'd be concerned for your mental health."

"You know what I mean, Lo. There's something we're missing. Some big piece we aren't seeing." He could tell Harlow was nervous. "People are out there, after this. For real. They really believe in whatever is in the Garden, don't they?"

Careful not to touch the skulls lining the walls, he moved to the side and allowed Harlow's brain to do what it did best—think.

Edward wanted to kiss her. Even among the skulls and other bones he didn't know the names of, Edward knew one thing for certain. He wanted to kiss her. But this...this was not good. He couldn't be in love with Harlow, not again. They had gone through too much already.

How was he supposed to make it all that go away?

"We need to go to Turkey."

"I'm sorry, what?"

"I need help to open the box. I understand where we're supposed to go I think. Do you remember—?"

"Yes."

"Hush." She smiled. "Do you remember the last page in the journal?"

"Of course." He closed his eyes.

"What word was written on it?"

"There was a sort of square with the word SIGNATUS inside it."

"Thought so. We need to go to Turkey."

"You mean the food?"

"The country, you moron." Harlow tried to hide a smile. "I need to visit a friend about some pre-Aramaic languages."

Chapter Twenty-Eight

"You aren't getting me on a plane," Edward stubbornly remarked.

"What?"

"I'm not flying to Turkey."

"Well, we sure as shit aren't walking there."

"Driving?"

"Trains."

"I don't drive trains."

"You..." Harlow playfully pushed Edward. He was caught off-guard, swayed too far to the right, and felt his entire arm rub against the wall of skulls, causing an immediate feeling of bile to rise in his throat. Oblivious, Harlow continued, "You don't drive the train. I meant as passengers. We can take the train to Turkey."

And so, less than five hours later, Edward found himself on a train to Turkey. He was thankful for the soft seats; his body ached for sleep.

"Say the plan again. Just one last time."

"We go to the temple, talk to Zion, solve the riddle, open the box, and get the next clue."

"Why do I feel like this is some national-treasure's-on-steroids bullshit," Edward mumbled from the seat next to Harlow.

"Because it is." Harlow shrugged. *Why was she so alert?* Edward wondered.

"Lo, they didn't follow us. You said it yourself; no one really knows about where we're headed. Why would the Germans follow us there?"

"It's not necessarily the Germans I'm worried about." She bit her lip.

Edward sighed and sat up. "Please don't tell me you murdered someone there and we're on a watch list in Turkey?"

"No! No, nothing like that." Lo wiggled nervously in her seat, making an odd squeaking noise. "I knew one of the monks is all. Zion."

"That's it? You knew some guy?" Edward paused. "Ah, if I had to bet, you flirted with this guy, and, now, you're worried that, going back, he's going to think it's more than a friendship, and you're worried if you have to flirt with him, that I'll be jealous and get mad."

"Also, I may have stolen their Bible."

"HARLOW!" Edward couldn't contain his voice. "I'm sorry? You stole the Bible from a group of ancient, religious monks?"

"Well, it was more like their pride and joy. You know, like the one remaining relic from the days of old."

"Ah. So you stole an ancient, sacred Bible from a group of religious monks, one of which you used to date. And, now, you want to go back and say 'hi,' borrow one of their sacred texts, all while a group of murderous thieves is chasing us?"

"The plan sounded better back at the catacombs before it was laid out like this."

"Any plan that sounds good, surrounded by dead people, is probably a bad plan to begin with." And so, Edward crossed his arms, turned toward the window in a failed attempt to force himself to sleep.

"All we have to do is open the box, find the next clue, and it'll make more sense." Harlow was too nervous to sleep.

"Why?" Edward opened his eyes. The world outside the window was dark, filled with houses whose lights were rapidly spinning by as their owners slept peacefully. Just how he wanted to be. Edward sat up and faced Harlow once more, trying not to show how upset he was getting. "Why do we need to open the box?"

"Seriously, Edward? Do you not understand that people are trying to find the Garden? You literally have been shot by someone after this."

"I was grazed by a bullet," he clarified. "And even if they did find the baptistery, Harlow, how would they find the next one?"

"What do you mean?"

"We have the next clue. Hell, we had the last one. What else is there to do but destroy these clues and walk away from it?" The frustration was showing now. There was no reason for this. How could the bad guys, let alone anyone, find the next clue now? It was impossible for them to find the clue, even if they had recorded down the entire notebook.

"No one knows the path to Eden if we destroy this." He held up the glittering box. "If we get rid of this and the journal and make sure no one has any more pages—"

"And what about Jane?" Harlow snapped. "Should we just leave her to die?"

"For all we know, she's already dead!" He regretted the words the second they left his mouth. "Lo, I didn't mean—"

"I don't have the journal," she cut him off, tears in the corner of her eyes. "I don't have it. After the fire at the mausoleum, I realized it was gone. I don't know if it was in the book bags or fell out somewhere…Edward, I don't have it."

Edward felt his heart thumping in his chest, and a hot sensation formed in his stomach.

The papers were gone. The bags were gone. And Jane was gone.

"I'm sorry, Ed. But this is what we have to do. We find the other clues, all of them, and we find Jane, and we do what Tiproil and Giovanni and every other person throughout history should have done: destroy them."

"But in doing so, you'll find Eden, won't you?"

Harlow nodded. "Yes. But there's a lot around that…there are rules, so to speak. They'll keep us safe. We can destroy the entrance so no one can ever find it."

"No," Ed said defiantly. "If all this is true, then let someone else destroy it. If the Garden of Eden exists, it's because God created it. He cast Adam and Eve out of it and set his angel to guard it. It's God's plan, not yours. Why should you be the one to go in and destroy centuries of history to keep safe what God already has?"

Harlow looked at Edward. She would be lying to him if she said she hadn't thought of this exact thing herself. She'd argued about it with Tiproil enough. If there was some massive cosmic entity out there who knew the master plan to the universe, shouldn't He have foreseen this arise?

"God does have a plan, Edward. We are that plan."

Chapter Twenty-Nine

The Sumela Monastery is located in Turkey and is just under 4,000 feet high, giving the appearance that it has been glued to a cliffside. Its soft, white color, flat, black roof, rectangular windows looking over the precipice with no emotion, gives it an eerie feel. It was thought to have been abandoned decades ago. An aqueduct reminds the few visitors of the thousand-year history hidden inside. Massive arches built from stones seem to stretch out their arms and welcome with a warning.

Harlow and Edward had arrived in the late evening. Exhausted from the train ride, they walked up the cliffside in the growing dusk, not saying much of anything to each other. By the time they got to the top, the sun had set fully, but they felt secure against the cliffside. Neither darkness nor height would shake the foundation.

"What happens when we get to the top?" Edward voiced his concern.

"They'll find us, don't worry," Harlow answered cryptically. "They probably know we're here already." She paused to tie the shoelace on her Chuck Taylors; they weren't the best for hiking, but, still, it could be worse.

Harlow and Edward carried on walking, approaching the stone structure of the Sumela Monastery. Suddenly, beams of light bobbed in the distance, growing larger. Edward grabbed Harlow's hand and pulled her behind his body for protection.

"Stop it," she argued. "They're fine."

Several hooded figures approached the exhausted duo.

"Then why are they wearing hoods?" he asked.

"You'd better be friendly, because we're too tired to fight," Edward's voice yelled out to the small group of men.

"I'm sorry about him." Lo pushed Edward aside and moved forward. "My name is Harlow. I've been here before."

Murmuring could be heard amongst the group of what Edward assumed were monks.

They seemed to be assessing the strange couple and making a decision if they could trust them.

Every beam of light remained focused on their faces, making it difficult to see clearly.

"I'm a friend of Zion's," Harlow spoke out.

Like magic, the monks lowered their lights and separated, making a path in between their bodies. One moved forward and lowered his hood, revealing a head of frizzy red hair and, to Edward's surprise, a woman.

"Follow me. Zion will be happy to see you, Harlow."

They walked inside the ancient walls and through a twisting, turning mash of buildings. Edward felt confused, even though he normally had a good sense of direction. It felt like old buildings were never torn down here, instead, they were mixed with new ones until the temple was this mesh of old and new, sitting on top of each other.

They came to a large room with vaulted ceilings. Another hooded figure stood across the length of the room; Edward assumed this was the famous Zion.

He watched from the stone wall nervously for what felt like hours. Lo was laughing with the hooded monk. He felt his stomach turn, and his face grew hot; who was this man she was talking to? How had they met? Was it before he knew her, or, worse, was it after?

Finally, knowing his mind couldn't take it anymore, he walked over and pulled Harlow aside by her arm. "Lo, this guy...he doesn't know anything."

Harlow smiled at his jealousy. "I know, Edward. *He* knows nothing." She took his hand in hers and led him over to where Zion was standing, hood still up, shrouding his face. "I would like you to meet Zion."

The man turned around and, with a gentle flick of his wrist, took down his hood. Edward wanted to punch Lo for her dramatics.

Zion was, in fact, a woman.

"Hello, Edward," Zion had a soft, low voice that hummed in tune with the monastery. Almost too perfectly connected with the surroundings for Edward to believe this was real life and not some ridiculous Indiana Jones film.

"Call me Ed, please, Your Holiness." He wasn't sure what to call her, but he felt someone with this much mystical aura needed a special title.

"I'm not the Pope, Edward. In fact, we are associated with a slightly different religion here at Sumela."

"Of course you are." He shrugged sarcastically. "Monks of the Hidden Garden?"

Zion raised an eyebrow and looked at Harlow quickly before glancing back at Edward.

"I'm the temple priest, Edward."

"Of course you are," he mumbled.

Harlow stepped forward, preventing Edward from continuing his blunder. "Zion, we've come for a reason. For the Garden..." She hesitated only for a moment before pulling the box out of her small bag. "We need your help with this. It must be solved. I believe the clue lies in your Holy Book."

"Hopefully not the Holy Book we do not have." A small smile slid across Zion's face.

"I was hoping you'd forgiven me for that..." Harlow's voice was meek. It wasn't often she had to come face to face with the people whose things she'd stolen.

"Are you asking for forgiveness?"

"I'm sorry, Zion, I should have never taken it."

There was a long moment of silence echoing eerily off the thick stone walls. "I read somewhere that the Codex is in the British Library now. Part of it at least—"

"Codex? I thought you stole a Bible?" Edward interjected.

"I swear, I had no idea they would separate it," the concern was harsh in Harlow's voice.

She turned to face Edward to quickly explain. "They refer to the oldest bibles as Codexes. Instead of scrolls, the words are written on both sides of paper, then folded up carefully in some sort of pattern that, when unfolded, is like turning the pages in a book. This one is written in Greek, and parts of it are now in exhibitions all over the world."

"They tore our book apart for the world to view it." Zion didn't sound upset; her monotone voice continued on evenly, "And, for that, we thank you, Harlow."

"What?" Both Lo and Edward exclaimed in unison.

"It was selfish of us to keep such history to ourselves."

Of course it was, Edward thought.

"You and your professor are right; the world deserves to know the truth. It may help some who have lost faith even."

Harlow's shoulders sagged. "The professor isn't with us anymore. He was...killed."

"I see. He is at peace now, Harlow. And that must be what brought you to our door after all these years?"

"Someone is trying to find Eden."

"You mean someone other than you and your professor? And, of course, him." Zion nodded toward Edward.

"He just works at a hardware store." She waved her hand to dismiss him.

"I manage. I manage hardware stores," he clarified. "But I used to do what Harlow does."

"Steal?"

"Reallocate."

Zion smiled at Edward.

"The Garden of Eden has never been found. Hundreds of thousands of years, and it has remained hidden. And not because it doesn't exist." Zion motioned for the two to follow her. "Thousands of years have passed since the dawn of mankind, and throughout history, there are links to a common ancestor."

"Adam and Eve?" Edward said skeptically.

"In a sense, yes. Take the story of Noah and the great flood. A similar version can be seen in Gilgamesh, one of the first written stories, centuries before Noah or Jesus or any of the authors of the Bible even lived."

"So you're saying parts of the Bible are plagiarized?"

"No, Edward." Zion laughed. "They're simply a different version of the same story, told for a different culture at a different time. But all the same nonetheless."

Doors spun open, and they descended down into a special super-secret room of mystery where the ancient codex was laid out under pressurized glass.

"The Garden of Eden is referred to across cultures and times. The dawn of the agricultural revolution was a Garden of Eden in part—when the first successful gardens provided everything a community needed with a surplus, culture erupted." Zion motioned to the dimly lit glass. "What Harlow has brought you here for, are these. The Dead Sea Scrolls."

"The what?" Edward had heard of these before, but he knew they weren't kept in a secret monastery carved into the side of a cliff. "These are supposed to be in museums."

"The terms 'Dead Sea Scrolls' references a collection of paper containing excerpts from the Bible found in a certain location. Archaeologists did not find them all. We have a few older ones here…"

"So there's the Dead Sea Scrolls and then what, the Deader Sea Scrolls?"

"I suppose you could say that." Zion smiled. "The scrolls are thought to be written close to the time of Jesus's death; some of the scrolls, we have predated them by a few years. We know because of several signatures. The most important being Jesus of Aramathea's." Silence hung in the air for a moment; ever Harlow was speechless.

"You have Jesus's actual signature," she whispered.

Zion simply nodded yes.

"OF COURSE YOU DO," Edward shouted. He couldn't identify the emotions he was feeling. Anger? Excitement? Disbelief? Utter surprise? Whatever was coursing through his veins, it was spiking his adrenaline levels and making him want to solve this mystery even more.

Zion led them over to a well-lit corner of the room where another airtight, humidity-controlled case was set up, the false lights glowing an odd, protective color of light down upon the ancient writings.

"The bottom right corner of the fifth page of the codex." Zion pointed, and Harlow and Edward's eyes snapped to the location where, sure enough, scribbled in deep black lines was a signature of sorts. Barely conscious of what he was doing, he pulled the box out from his pocket.

Harlow reached over and began sliding the mosaic pieces around. Sure enough, the signature began to form among the little black lines running through the tiles on the box. They aligned perfectly and, just like some holy miracle, a clicking noise could be heard; out slid a piece of paper.

Edward scooped up the paper and gently unfolded it while Harlow studied the box, making sure the contents had been entirely emptied. Content the paper was the only secret held in the box, she turned her attention to it.

Harlow's voice came out in only a whisper, "It's a map."

Chapter Thirty

"A map? They give us an old map?! We came this far, and they chose NOW to give us a damned map?" Edward was furious. Harlow held her breath, unsure of what the next clue meant.

Tiproil had never mentioned an actual map before. Was it a trick?

"What does it look like exactly?" even Zion's calm voice seemed slightly strained. "I believe it is a Beatice Map, but older." No one bothered to ask what a Beatice Map was. Edward had a hunch it was going to be something dealing with historical people searching for Eden and putting it on their maps.

The group stared intently at the ancient paper with its symbols and arrows drawn around. It could be no longer than a foot widthwise, height even less. The edges were crumbling, a testament to its age, and the fold lines were causing even more damage at their intersections with each other.

Up in the right-hand corner were two small trees, their once ink-green leaves faded to almost brown, encircled by a thick black line. Other lines clearly denoted mountains and cities at the time; four, faded, blue rivers flowed out of the corner where the trees were.

"Memorize it," Harlow barked the order at Edward. "We're burning it after you do."

"What?" Both Zion and Edward said in unison.

"We can't risk anyone finding this map. Whatever it leads to, it eventually leads to Eden." She pointed to the two trees in their small circle. "A direct map anyone can uncover and decipher? We need to keep Eden hidden, not let everyone in the world be led right to it."

Edward understood her. The map he held was arguably the most dangerous thing in the world. What if it fell into the wrong hands like those of Margo and the other people chasing them? They had kidnapped Jane and, for all they knew, killed her. Who else would suffer on their quest to find Eden?

Zion spoke, her voice back to its usual softness, "I do not think it leads directly to Eden. Look down at the city circled in the same way Eden is. It has a strange shape drawn next to it." Sure enough, there was a sort of pointed rectangle scribbled next to the city that was clearly not meant to be a building. "I think that is where the map leads us to."

"What the hell is that supposed to be?" Edward pointed to squiggly black lines above the circular city. They looked like chicken scratch in some type of tribal design.

"That's cuneiform!" Harlow exclaimed. "The world's oldest writing system. Older than hieroglyphics, this takes us back to before Christ, before the Common Era..." Harlow's breath was short with excitement. "Zion, do you know where this is?"

"The city of Uruk," she spoke quietly.

"Anyone care to explain the significance?" Edward sighed. As much as he disliked Jane, it would be nice to have someone alongside who despised these lectures as much as he did. But she was not here, and he knew the knowledge was necessary.

"It's thought to be the oldest city on Earth, not to mention the most powerful at one point in time. It's where writing was first invented, the first ziggurat—a type of temple," Harlow added extra clarity for Edward. "It's also where Gilgamesh was said to live. The epic tale is thought to be the first story ever written. It's about a great king; it has similarities to the stories in the Bible. A great flood, the king's quest for immortality…"

"And I bet there's something about a garden there too." Both women nodded yes.

"Great. So we go to Urek or whatever it's called and find what exactly?"

"Uruk. And I don't know," Harlow admitted. "Tiproil and I had talked about what we might find along the way, but we never talked about Uruk." Harlow seemed to be debating something in her mind, going back and forth between what to say next and how to say it, and if she should even say it out loud or keep it to herself. "The papers will say what we have to look for."

"I knew they'd be important beyond the first clues!" Edward smiled. "That's why we were keeping them safe. Okay, so we look at the papers, figure out what we need to find, then go to Urak and find it."

"Uruk," Zion corrected him. "And I don't think it'll be that easy."

"Why not?" Edward looked from Zion to Harlow, searching for an answer to the cryptic comment. "Just look at the papers, they'll tell us." His remark went unanswered; silence hung in the air.

"Lo, where are the papers?" Edward asked. A sliver of ice went down his spine as an awful realization sunk in. Why hadn't he seen them lately? They hadn't been in his hands since back before Italy. "Lo, where are the papers?" he asked once more, but he knew the answer in her silence.

"You wouldn't lose them; I know this," anger grew in his voice. "But you would destroy them. Just like you're willing to burn this map. You set the papers on fire, didn't you?" Harlow still was silent.

"DIDN'T YOU?" he screamed.

"They needed to be disposed of safely. Tiproil had said—"

"Oh, I'm so sick of you and your precious professor. How many hundreds of people are after the Garden now that he opened his mouth?"

"Stop it. You're just jealous—"

"Jealous!? You think I'm jealous? Harlow, I'm in Turkey, a country I had no desire to EVER visit—no offence, Zion—with some raving mad Germans chasing me down; I killed a man, got shot, and you think I'm JEALOUS of a dead professor?"

"I think you're glad he's dead," Harlow's voice was hollow.

"No, I think you're guilty that he's dead, and you're guilty you pulled us into this." Edward heard Zion take a breath as if to separate herself out from the grouping. She was not at all upset Harlow had involved her. Suddenly, he realized what he had done in his anger; he had temporarily broken her with his words.

"The papers are gone. That's all you need to know." Pulling out a lighter, she quickly set fire to the ancient map they had searched so long for and tossed it on the stone floor, watching it burn. Lo had shut down all emotions; any outlet that would lead to learning more about what she had done or how she was feeling was closed off. There would be no more from her tonight.

Chapter Thirty-One

The drive to Uruk was violently silent; resentment and frustration seemed to jostle around the armored car with each pothole they ran over. Zion had arranged a private flight from Turkey to Iraq, much to Edward's protests. They were heading for Uruk, aiming to visit the archaeological site and, in Zion's words, find some type of divine intervention which would lead them on from there.

Edward was exhausted. He was confused. He was a million emotions bottled into one, old, tired body. He had no idea what to expect once they got to the temple site; did Harlow think Jane would be there? In his opinion, they should have searched the local hospitals to find Jane, but Harlow seemed secure in her argument Margo and the rest of the baddies would be taking Jane with them on their hunt. But how would they know to head to Uruk? They wouldn't. The closer he, Harlow, and Zion got to the primordial city, the further away they were from finding Jane.

"Uruk has many layers to it. The city has existed for thousands of years, beginning around five-thousand B.C."

"Does it exist now?" Edward asked.

"For all intent and purpose, no. There is a modern-day city but it's far enough away from the archaeological site;

we won't have to worry about it much." Harlow led them out of the parked car and through the early morning air toward a fairly well-lit, large pile of dirt.

"That's where the clue for the magical Garden of Eden is hidden?" Disbelief was rampant on Edward's face. "I expected the temple to at least be standing."

"A ziggurat is a steep pyramid," Harlow began to explain.

"It is layers of dirt piled atop each other," Zion summarized the important part.

Sure enough, the closer they got to the archaeological site, the clearer it became: the ziggurat was piles and piles of dirt.

"Let's look at the tents first." Harlow motioned to a row of large, white tents set up near the dig site. They served as buildings of sorts for the scientists and workers at the site. "Anything interesting they found would be here or at a lab," she added sheepishly.

"So, if we don't find the next magical clue here, we're screwed," Edward summarized this time.

"Perhaps luck will be on our side," Zion spoke in her soft voice.

"Aren't you supposed to not believe in luck?" Edward tested her.

"Luck, blessings, all the same thing. A gift from the Lord, whatever you call it." Zion smiled.

"Okay. One of these tents will have what we're looking for. The normal order of sites like this is dig, search, and anything interesting gets recorded then brought here where it's packed up to get sent back to a processing lab."

Edward sighed. As much as he disliked the Indiana Jones feeling he got from this whole adventure, searching through bags of dirt for something that might relate to the Garden of Eden seemed like an even worse prospect.

The large tents were close to the base of the ziggurat. Large tables were set up with white paper bags on top of them. Arabic written in black marker on each bag denoted where the artifact was found and other information no one could read. Several parked cars were next to the tents. As Edward surveyed the sight, he saw barrels of what he suspected were gasoline piled next to them. They were in Iraq, not the United States; O.S.E.A. had no control over worksites here.

The trio began searching for a vague something in the growing light. Thankfully, the area was deserted, but as dawn approached, it wouldn't stay that way for long. An hour passed in relative silence with only an odd comment or two from Harlow.

"What are you finding?" she asked.

"Pottery." Zion sighed softly. "Lots of pottery."

"Me too. At least I think." Edward had the most opened bags surrounding him, as he was unceremoniously opening and throwing them in any direction once empty, blatantly ignoring one of Harlow's comments regarding 'keeping the integrity of the dig site.'

Harlow and Zion walked over to Edward's pile. Harlow bit her tongue as the two began searching through Edward's pile of 'stuff.'

"Strange, this is all thousands of years old, and we are just rifling through it like a rummage sale," Zion observed.

"Maybe the ancient people thought it was junk too," Edward remarked. He pulled a bag out at random from the large pile on the table next to him and opened it. A strange bracelet of black beads fell out.

"Well, this is cool." He held up his find.

"That's incredible." Harlow took it from his hands gently. "They're obsidian beads. How they survived, intact this whole time…"

"Obsidian is a volcanic glass. Extremely sharp when cut correctly, but it can also break easily." Once again, Zion summarized what was in Harlow's brain.

"Well, the knife thing survived too." Edward held up a black knife no longer than his hand. It was covered in dirt, but it was clearly an obsidian knife.

"Harlow, what was the shape drawn next to the city or Uruk on the map we burnt? Was it not…" Zion didn't need to finish her sentence. All the pieces began to fall into place.

"The angel at the east guarded the gates with a sword of fire," she paraphrased from the Bible. "Sword of fire. Maybe it isn't a sword of fire at all, but a sword *from* fire. An obsidian blade; volcanic glass."

"Perhaps this is what we are searching for."

"The papers knew what we were looking for. Harlow, give me a pen," Edward ordered.

"Why would I have a pen on me?" Harlow put her hands up in the air. The only thing she had were the clothes on her back and the Chuck Taylors on her feet. Zion quickly snatched a marker from one of the tables and handed it to Edward. He wrote frantically on an empty bag.

'Superare necesse flammeum gladium angeli custodes paradise.'

"The papers had a line something like this. It was on the fifth page toward the bottom, written almost like an afterthought. I don't know if I got the spelling right, but the main point is there. What does it say?"

"A sword of fire is needed to defeat the angel that guards the Garden," Zion spoke with no hesitation. Her Latin wasn't rusty at all.

It was then the world seemed to wake up. Three busses pulled into the dig site, parking alongside their armored car. The busses unloaded what felt like hundreds of workers who moved like ants in lines toward the ziggurat. Dressed in light, linen clothes with head coverings, it was evident the three intruders did not belong. They ducked down beneath one of the tables, all three of them knowing it was a terrible hiding spot.

"We have stayed long enough," Zion said quietly. "We must walk to the car and drive away."

"We don't know where to go," Harlow was bitter. "The clues are all messed up."

"Well, good. Then we destroy the sword/dagger thing and no one ever finds Eden," Edward remarked. This was it. He was so close to being done with their insane task; almost at the finish line. He could go back home to his beer and rebuild his gazebo.

A bus full of tourists pulled up; a mix of accents and languages could be heard as they got off the bus and headed toward the ziggurat.

"We blend in with them and walk to the car," the words barely left Zion's mouth when the distinct sound of a gun being cocked drew their attention behind them. Margo, her red hair blowing in the dry wind, was standing with her gun pointed at the trio.

"Give me the dagger," Margo spoke English with her strange accent. She turned to Sam and Georg, her two gun-wielding henchmen, and spoke orders to them in another language.

"What language did you think they spoke?" Zion asked.

"German," Edward answered.

"Not German, Africans. They're from South Africa," Zion corrected him matter-of-factly.

"Good to know, but not entirely helpful at a time like this," Edward muttered. He stepped sideways, closer to Harlow. It was pure instinct to protect her.

Before anyone had a chance to utter another word, Zion fired two gunshots, one hitting Sam directly in the head, the other hitting Margo in her side. Margo fired back, missing her targets completely but causing harm just the same.

The noise of the bullet being fired could barely be heard through the silencer on the gun, but the result of a high-speed projectile rupturing gasoline barrels was an enormous explosion that sent Edward and Harlow flying through the air. Zion's body disappeared in the blaze.

Chapter Thirty-Two

Edward wasn't sure if screams of terror sounded more urgent in Arabic or English, but he was certain that regardless of language, panic sounded the same. He found himself searching for an unconscious Harlow who looked worse than she actually was. Thankfully, in all the chaos, the three of them were the last suspects, simply kind yet naive tourists who wanted to help.

Harlow was beginning to come around; Edward pushed away the never-ending sea of hands reaching out to help in some way.

"She's fine! We're fine! Just need some air!" He wished he knew Arabic. "Leave us alone!" That one seemed to work slightly. He still felt pushing and shoving as the crowd grew around them and around the site. Particles of dirt still floated in the air, making it hazy and hard to breathe.

"Sorry about this, Lo," Edward mumbled. He tossed her up over his shoulder so her head hung down his back. His mind fluttered back to a year ago in Harlow's townhouse. It was one of the last times they saw each other, but neither knew it would be significant. They only argued through laughter about things that never really mattered. Edward settled the matter by flinging Harlow over his shoulder, like he had her now, and carrying her up the stairs into the bedroom where he tossed her on the bed and proceeded to kiss her like mad until she succumbed to a smile.

Edward carried her limp body away from the detonation site, away from the crowd of people trying to see what had happened. Softly setting Harlow down on a bench near the busses, he tried to catch his breath. He was getting too old for this sort of thing.

The yells across the site were drowned out by sirens now as police cars and fire trucks appeared on the scene. It wouldn't be long before some clever detective began piecing it together, realizing that the strange foreigners poking around the dig site might be more involved than previously thought.

"Lo, you've have to get up. Zion is somewhere, hurt. This would really be much easier and less suspicious if you were walking next to me instead of you thrown over my shoulder."

"If you learned how to catch me the right way, I wouldn't have to continuously get concussions," Harlow's quiet voice grumbled, her eyes still closed.

"You're alive!" Edward leaned over excitedly and began kissing her forehead. To hell with Eden; he was happy Harlow was alive.

"Hey, possible concussion here."

"Sorry, sorry." He leaned back, his hands helping her to sit up slowly. "How's the head?"

"Sore." Harlow closed her eyes. She could feel her pulse pounding in her temples. "The obsidian!"

"I have it." He reached into his pocket but didn't pull out the small knife.

"As long as we have the knife." Harlow watched the chaos unfolding across the dig site.

She knew they should go, but she quite liked sitting close to Edward on this bench, his arm instinctively and protectively around her. They used to be like this all the time before she left; she hated to admit exactly how much she missed him.

He was barely aware of his arm still being around Harlow, only really noticing he felt oddly comfortable given the scene of pandemonium.

"Harlow, Jane doesn't just speak English, does she?"

"No."

"What language does she speak?"

"Africans. She used to live in South Africa once upon a time. Why?" It all made sense now.

"It's Jane. Jane is—"

"Jane is getting sick and tired of this game," the assassin's voice cracked through the air like a whip. Her blonde hair contrasted against Margo's red hair as the two women held out their guns with shaking hands. It was their injuries that caused this, not their lack of will to use them, Edward noted.

Clutched tightly in the free hand of Margo was Zion, badly burnt and barely alive.

"Take me to the next location, or the nun dies."

"Actually, she's a temple priest," Edward spat. He should have known. He never liked Jane anyway.

"I don't care what she is. She's going to be dead soon unless you take me to the next location."

"We don't know where it is!" Harlow yelled. She was in shock.

"Of course you do. If it isn't in your brain." Jane shook her gun at Harlow. "Then it's in his memory." She pointed to Edward.

"Stop it, Jane. He doesn't know. You think he can understand what is in his mind?" Harlow was close to tears.

Zion could barely stand, and Margo was beginning to struggle in holding all her weight. *She's dying*, Edward thought. There was no way for her body to last much longer after it withstood such an intense trauma.

"You tell me what the next clue is, or she dies." Jane cocked her gun and pushed it painfully against Zion's burnt head. There was dried blood on Jane's head from her fall back in Italy. In the hand not holding the gun against Zion's head, Jane held a large paper map.

"You aren't listening, Jane. He doesn't know where the next location is. Neither of us do." Harlow was crying now. Zion appeared to be unconscious in Margo's arms.

"It's in my head, Lo. The map…" Edward closed his eyes and searched his memory for what he knew was there. He just didn't know what it meant, what any of it meant.

"There's a symbol, like a tree, drawn on the map. There's the number 70 written next to a tree symbol inside a circle, and the letters N.W."

"70 paces North West I bet," Lo had spoken before she could stop herself. "I need a modern day map and Edward's memory."

Scuffling could be heard as Jane brought the map to where Edward was standing.

"Here and here." Edward pointed to two locations on the map that was sprawled out on the hood of their car. His voice was bitter.

"Gobekli Tepe," Harlow whispered. "Of course it's there…"

"Where is it?" Jane's voice was high-pitched and excited. "Where are we going?"

"To the oldest manmade temple on Earth, of course."

"Need me." Edward scoffed, suddenly thinking of Harlow's words. He stared at her crying face, and she saw nothing but ice in his eyes. "You don't need me, Lo. You've never needed me. You lied to me." Silence set went silent as Edward's voice rang out, "*Need* me, you've never needed me a day in your life; you said it yourself: 'I do everything by myself.' And, yet, here you are, suddenly saying you need me. You don't need me, you're using me. That's all this ever was, isn't it?"

Edward knew he was right. She used him to get what she wanted. Neither he nor Jane know Latin, so they had no idea if the words from the journal were used in the first translation or if there were some left over. It all made sense now. After they figured out how to get to Ravenna, Harlow went and destroyed the papers—actually, she destroyed them in the fire of the mausoleum, if he had to bet on it. Jane tried to look for the papers but couldn't find them, so she stuck around until she was sure there was no more than what they had. The fall might have been an accident, but nothing else was.

Jane seemed unbothered by Edward's revelation. She pulled the trigger, and what was left of Zion's skin split open as the bullet ripped through her skull. Her lifeless body fell against the ground.

"Take me to Gobekli Tepe."

Chapter Thirty-Three

Gobekli Tepe stands, to this day, as the oldest manmade temple in the world, older than even Stonehenge by 6,000 years.

The darkness was lit up by floodlights shining upward from the earth, casting an unearthly glow on massive stone pillars that stood the test of time. Intricate carvings of animals danced in a spectral show, echoing the ghosts of the past as the group lowered themselves down into the circular temple.

Edward knew he didn't have to know much about archaeology or history to know this place was sacred and old, and if Eden was going to be hidden anywhere, it was under the remains of this site.

"Lo, stay by me." He was overcome with an urge to keep her close and to keep her safe.

He didn't trust this place.

"It's holy! You can feel it." Jane was spinning in circles, her blonde hair twirling behind her as she tried to take it all in. "You can almost see Adam and Eve carving their story in the stone. The animals of Eden, the warnings of God…"

"It would've been their tribe, not just them," Harlow muttered bitterly.

"Where do we go? How do we find the entrance?" Margo looked to Jane as she asked but knew it was Harlow and Edward who would have the answers.

"'And God said, 'See, the man has become like one of us, knowing good and evil. Now, to prevent his putting out his hand and taking also from the tree of life, eating, and living forever—' So, he drove out the man, and he placed at the east of the garden of Eden cherubims, and a flaming sword which turned every way, to keep the way of the tree of life.'" Harlow took a breath. For a moment, Edward thought she might cry. "Almost all the versions of Genesis, even the Jewish ones, say something similar. The circular shape of the temple refers to 'turning every which way' and guarding the Tree."

"Circles have no end and no beginning. No weaknesses. The best kind of defense." Jane was eager to continue the decoding. "So we look east?"

"How do you find east in a circle?" Harlow smirked. "A circle has no point of north, therefore no east."

"But the Bible says—"

"The Bible also references four rivers, Jane. Do you see them rushing by?" The whistling wind whipping dirt around their faces was the only response. "11-thousand years is a long time." She turned to face two of the largest standing pillar-like statues, their faces over 16 feet up in the air, worn away by that time.

"We're looking for a cherubim." Harlow closed her eyes and reached out to touch the ancient stone as she thought. The professor's face flashed across her racing mind. How often had they discussed angels? Why a cherubim?

Chapter Thirty-Four

Six years earlier.

"Another email from the dean. Harlow, you broke into the newsroom and managed to reprint every university newspaper to discuss corruption on campus?" Snow had melted, and spring was around the corner. The campus was bursting with the stress of final studying being crammed in time that no one had in their schedule.

"How does the dean know it was me?"

"She doesn't. I do." He tossed the newspaper on top of his desk. "Photocopies of receipts from professors' reimbursement statements. The only place they're kept is on file in the financial office, and in all my time here, I only know of one student who managed to successfully slip into locked offices."

"People deserve to know if their tuition money goes to refund a man for spending $300.00 on a bottle of whiskey."

"It was scotch, and I agree with you that this type of fiscal irresponsibility is unjust—"

"I was simply relaying the facts."

"They're calling it *hijacking*…"

"I call it freedom of speech."

"Harlow!" He slammed his fist onto his desk. "I don't think you understand the seriousness of this. The police are getting involved. People are going to lose their jobs. One professor you named has already fled the country. Expulsion for this type of thing—"

"On what grounds will they expel me?" Harlow sat down in her usual spot.

"I am a proponent for education." Tiproil relaxed slightly in his worn office chair. "That being said, I am an even larger proponent for uncovering your calling in life."

"What are you trying to say?"

Tiproil understood parts of Harlow. He couldn't quite explain how, as he had never gone through what she had, nor had he known anyone quite like her. But he knew her future lay outside of the university walls. Her skills were not meant for nine-five office hours, and 401Ks would not be what she based her retirement off of.

"You think I should leave, don't you?" Harlow could barely believe she had said those words.

"I didn't say that."

"But you're thinking it. You just want me to steal this shit for you so you don't have to get your hands dirty, don't you?" Harlow felt her temper rise.

"Harlow, absolutely not. It's getting more and more difficult to cover for you. I've been in six behavioral meetings with the dean since the start of the semester."

"I'm not failing any of my classes; why on earth would the dean—"

"Harlow! Think! The university is built on more than just good grades from its students. If word got out that a future alumni was—"

"I get it," Harlow said bitterly. "You don't have to say out loud that you know I'm a thief. I get it. I don't belong here."

"I'm not saying you don't *belong*; I'm only saying your talents might be more useful elsewhere." He wanted her to understand, but the more he spoke, the further away she drifted.

A robin landed on the bush just outside Tiproil's window. It stood still, looking at the window pane as if deciding whether it should attempt to pass through the glass. Realizing the world outside was nicer, it turned its red belly away from the eyes of those inside the office and began chirping a soft song.

"I thought you needed me here, helping you with Eden," Harlow's voice was quiet.

"We have all the papers." Tiproil braced himself before he said the next few words.

"Only one copy remains."

"What?" Harlow jumped to her feet. "What do you mean 'only one remains'? This isn't some cryptic bullshit, *Yoda*, I stole—"

"You stole six copies. I know. They were the only six copies in the world, besides the one now hidden in the safety deposit box I own."

"You…you tricked me!" Harlow felt the sharp stab of an all-too-familiar betrayal slice through her body. "You said I was helping you."

"And you were. You ARE helping me." Tiproil stood slowly. He was getting older, and it had begun to show. "I couldn't have collected those papers on my own. I couldn't have done all that research on my own either. You found the last two papers after all."

"But why, I don't understand." Harlow looked at Tiproil's brown eyes, so similar to her own. "I don't understand…" She began to cry softly.

"No one can know what the papers contain." Tiproil was fighting with his mind, Harlow could tell. He was wondering how much he should disclose. "You read all my work, Harlow. You know almost everything I know. Except for the papers and the cypher; it's the first clue to Eden."

Harlow's attention immediately snapped into focus. "The first clue? The beginning of it all?" Both were silent, their minds mulling over what was happening. "I looked at them. Every single one I stole, I looked over before giving them to you, even though I told you I hadn't looked. But there's not much there…they're full of numbers and words and pictures. A ledger of sorts. I never thought…" She paused. "I never thought you were, what, burning them as I brought them to you?"

Tiproil nodded yes. "I should have told you earlier. I see now you can be trusted. I was just so worried…so worried that if you knew I was destroying the papers, you wouldn't help me find and collect them." They sat together in silence for the last time in Tiproil's office, although neither knew it would be the last.

"It's better this way. Now no one has the papers; no one knows about the cypher, but, more importantly—"

"No one will ever find Eden," Lo finished his sentence with a bored tone. She had heard him say it nearly a thousand times by now. No one must ever find Eden. The words were drilled into her head every day. "I understand, Tiproil. It's important no one discovers it."

Chapter Thirty-Five

Harlow thought back to Tiproil's office and all the times she had spent sitting in that chair that didn't quite fit the room. How much work they had gone over, how many books and websites they had sifted through to collect what information they could on Eden. She knew which one the cherub was— the stone guardian with a lion carved into it. It was easy to remember. She could remember every meeting in his office that smelt of tangerines and ink. She could remember him with his dark eyes and stern voice. But she couldn't bring herself to think of him dead; in her mind, he was alive and well and sitting at his desk, typing some email on his computer right now.

Harlow walked over to the lion and studied it. Down near its belly is a small crevice, small enough to simply look like a crack and nothing more. But Harlow knew better; this was deliberate.

"The east," Harlow muttered to herself. "The east." The east had to be important. It wouldn't be mentioned in *every* translation to not be important. Tiproil had to be wrong in his thinking that it meant nothing. What happened in the east?

"The sunrise." Harlow took a step back. "The sun rises in the east. Always has, always will. Even before we knew what direction to call it, we knew the sun would rise in that direction." She ran over and grabbed a floodlight from the ground. "Ed, help me with this!"

Jane and Margo stood by, watching the two struggle to move the large light, their guns still poised for added security. Jane hated to admit it, but she couldn't help but marvel at how smart Harlow was. Not many people would think to fake the sunrise.

"Give me the obsidian." Harlow held out her hand; the stone felt cold as Jane placed it in her warm hands. As the spotlight shone brightly on the stone statue, Harlow walked forward with the sword of fire. She set the tip against the crack and hesitated. Here was Eden. Tiproil was dead. She was being forced to enter the place she'd dreamt of so many nights. How had things turned so wrong?

She felt another hand steady hers and opened her eyes to see Edward standing next to her.

"We do this together…but, Harlow, what if this is like *Raiders of the Lost Ark*?"

"What?" Her brain was too flooded with emotions to comprehend what he was saying.

"The Indiana Jones movie!"

"For the last time, Ed, this is real life—"

"That's why I'm saying this!" his whispers were urgent now. "This is real, Lo. All of it. Eden is real. And so is that tree. You go in there and eat it. You might turn to goo like the people did when they looked on the Ark of the Covenant."

"I wouldn't turn into goo. I would be struck down by God in some way," her reply was calm, like she had known death was eminent from the beginning. "But we do it anyway. I can't let you die, and I can't let Margo or Jane get in without someone to stop them."

And with those words, Edward and Harlow pushed the sword back to its home with the cherubim of stone. They felt a click as it locked into place.

Everyone waited with bated breath, but nothing happened. No spinning transport to another dimension, no flash of colors and blinding light, no earth-opening cavern beneath them.

Nothing but the same rocks staring back.

The floodlight shone onto everything, casting an eerie light across the ancient sculpture. For a moment, nothing happened, and then a loud crack could be heard. Then, without warning, the ground began to shake. A smashing, grinding noise caused everyone to grab their ears. Stone scraped upon stone, and ropes could be heard snapping from a distance, perhaps underfoot.

The stone guardian slipped downward into the earth. Harlow grabbed the boxed lights and tilted them toward the black abyss. There were uneven steps leading downward into the earth; this was the path to Eden.

Chapter Thirty-Six

The tunnel was narrow, and Harlow didn't want to go into it. The gun held against her back by Margo suggested otherwise. It was dusty and rocky and cramped; the group moved painstakingly slowly as they marched through it. Edward felt the gun held by Jane pushing into his shoulder blades as they rounded a corner.

If they survived this, he could never go back to working at the hardware store. Being a manager, that boring mundane life, just wouldn't cut it anymore. He could no longer deny that he loved this—regardless of how complicated the situation was right now and the potential for imminent death—he loved Harlow and the adventure she brought along with her. He wanted a life with her. Strange to realize it at a time like this where they were marching at gunpoint toward certain death.

As the curve straightened out, the tunnel grew larger until it was a cavern and the group was standing at the entrance to an underground world. The cave stretched beyond their eyesight, but, oddly enough, they could see what was in front of them without needing flashlights.

Edward looked up and saw strange crystals glowing from the roof of the cavern. They glinted and glimmered, shining light down below. A stone arch stood at least ten feet high and half as wide across directly in their path.

Hesitantly, Jane and Margo pushed Edward and Harlow forward. Behind the archway, they saw a rolling green hill with trees atop it. Harlow felt something running down her cheek; her hand reached up and wiped a tear away. She had finally done it. They had found the Garden of Eden.

Jane pushed Edward forward, ignorant of the special moment Harlow was having. "You go through the arch first."

"You're scared." Harlow turned toward her former friend. "All this time, and you're scared to go into the Garden?"

"Shut up." Jane pointed her gun toward Harlow for only a moment, then quickly shifted it back toward Edward. He looked desperately at Harlow. There were so many things he wanted to tell her. What if he never got the chance? What if he wasn't meant to be with her? What if fate had brought them here only to die in this sacred place?

He took a determined step forward. For Harlow, he would brave through this disaster, and if he died in the journey, then so be it.

"NO!" Harlow's voice echoed through the holy place, smashing through the silence. "I'll go. Put the guns down. I'll go get you your fruit." What was she doing, Edward wondered.

Her Chuck Taylors barely made a sound on the mossy ground. She took one step and then another. Soon, she was through the arch and saw the sprawling field around her and the graceful rise of the hill. She began to walk upward, feeling the ground squelch underneath her feet. She looked down to see mud and a small sliver of water trickling across the ground.

"The water still flows," Harlow spoke in a whisper. A scientist would have looked at the ground and deduced that the trickle was once a large flowing river and that the years had lessened its stream, killing off and changing much of the flora and fauna in the region. Be that as it may, Harlow and the group were just floored such a cave even existed. It went on for miles, trees and other plants blooming in all directions.

The further into the Garden she went, the stranger it became. The grove of trees grew thicker, but Harlow wasn't worried. She and Tripoli had never discussed what the tree would look like per se, but Harlow knew the tree she was looking for. Right in the center of the Garden, among hundreds of trees, two stood taller than the rest, surrounded by a circle of mossy rocks.

"There's the Tree of Knowledge of Good and Evil and the Tree of Life," Harlow recited their names like she had done a thousand times in Tiproil's office. "It is forbidden to eat from the Tree of Life," Harlow said matter-of-factly. "It's written, and it must be disobeyed apparently." She walked forward and heard the crunch of skeletons strewn across the ground. Animals had died in the Garden, unable to live with the changing climate.

Harlow reached up and picked what looked like a fig off of the tree. She held it in her hand and thought of Tripoli. He wanted this moment, had studied, strived, and struggled for this moment, and here she was while he was dead. It didn't seem fair, but it was fate.

Jane walked back and forth, her gun swinging wildly from her hand. "I should have never let her go in alone. If she doesn't come back in five more minutes, you're dead." She looked over at Edward.

"That's not fair. You never gave her a time limit. She'll be back. Just let her figure it out. There's hundreds of trees in there." Edward tried to ignore the gun Margo continued to point at him. Harlow would find the right tree; there was no other option, because he didn't plan to die today.

Edward needed to keep Jane talking. "Why did you do it? Why turn on her? Was it money? Is someone paying you?"

Jane stopped pacing and turned to face Edward. She moved her face close to his and whispered her confession. "It's never about money, Ed. It's about who has power and who needs it."

Suddenly, in the distance, they saw the figure of Harlow emerge from the grove of trees.

Edward knew at once she was holding the fruit.

Jane couldn't wait for the figure to grow any larger. She took off, running through the gates, but stumbled. Her feet seemed unable to hold her weight. Harlow rushed forward toward her; by the time she got there, Jane had collapsed on the ground.

"Don't come in!" Harlow yelled at Edward and Margo. "There's something weird here. Some kind of force field surrounding the Garden."

Edward couldn't believe it; a force field? He couldn't wrap his head around some supernatural force protecting the Garden. But, then again, all of this was happening because of a fruit tree with the ability to give everlasting life.

He began to walk slowly through the gates but felt something pushing him back. Maybe she was right and there was some type of force field preventing him from passing through. What if Harlow was right and Jane couldn't get through because she was corrupt in spirit? But if that were the case, then why would Harlow be unaffected?

Edward stood at the gate and waited for Harlow to finish pulling Jane across the threshold. Margo stood with the gun limp in her hand, dumbfounded at the scene playing out before her.

"She'll be fine once she gets out of the Garden," Harlow said.

"Give me the fruit," Jane's voice was raspy and harsh. She clawed at Harlow's arms, trying to stand and snatch the fruit all at once.

"Calm down," Harlow replied. They stumbled across the gate, and Jane took a vicious breath of air. It was as if a weight had been lifted off her chest. "Take a breath and let your body adjust."

"Give it to me!" Jane knelt before Harlow, her gun tossed beside her on the mossy ground. All she cared about was the fruit.

Harlow calmly handed Jane the garnet-colored fruit and her fingers greedily closed around it.

"I eat this, and I live forever?" She didn't bother to stand.

"Like God never intended." Harlow nodded yes. "Adam and Eve ate from the other tree, but God cast them out of here before they could eat this."

"It looks so…normal…" Margo whispered.

"You sure about this, Lo?" Edward asked, clearly in agreement with Margo. What could Harlow be thinking? Why would she willingly let Jane eat the fruit?

"I'm sure," Harlow answered sternly.

Before she finished speaking, Jane opened her mouth to take a bite. Harlow never hesitated. Her face stone-cold and stoic, she took a step forward, brandishing a sliver of obsidian, flaked from the sword the cherubim held. Barely a sound was heard as Jane's neck was slit open, the obsidian quickly pulled back out. Her blood was the color of the fruit's skin; it fell in spurts on the grass where her body landed without another word.

Harlow leaned down and picked up the gun from the ground and the fruit from Jane's dead hands. She turned toward Edward and Margo.

In an instant, Margo understood the game was over. She put both her hands up in surrender, shock written all over her face. "You let me go, I walk away. Jane was the only reason I was here. I believed in her and her money and, now, there's nothing left there. Just let me go." She took a step backward toward the entrance of the cave.

"If you go, will you tell anyone?"

"I'll take the secret of Eden to my grave," Margo was convincing, but she was scared.

Before she could utter another testament, a gunshot rang out through the garden.

Harlow sighed.

Margo's body crumpled to the ground, a bullet hole in her head.

"I'm sorry, Edward." Harlow turned from the dead girl. Her shoulders slumped as she spoke again, "It's just that she—"

"I know. She was lying." Edward looked up at Lo as she stood near the stone gate, the entire Garden of Eden sprawling behind her. An idea suddenly crossed his mind. This wasn't the end of everything with Harlow; he wanted it to be the beginning. "What if we stayed?"

Lo smiled and looked down at the fruit in her hand. "The Garden wasn't made for people to hide in. There's a whole world out there we need to live in." She would be lying if she had said she wasn't tempted to stay, and Edward knew it. This was one of the most difficult decisions, to walk away. But it had to be done. God never intended anyone to live in the Garden forever. Adam and Eve left for a reason; Harlow knew she and Edward had to as well.

They set the bodies besides the stone wall. Harlow left Edward behind and passed through the gate once more, making one final climb to the grove of trees, the blood fruit still in her hands. With trembling fingers that wanted to disobey her heart, she set the fruit on the ground by the foot of the tree, stood up, and walked back toward Edward.

They turned their backs and, together, walked out of Eden, leaving the cherub with his sword of fire to guard the gate once more.

Epilogue

Tiproil was a man of many mysteries, but as Harlow knew, it only ever took one simple explanation to have it all make sense. Why did he publish his findings? Harlow had wondered the same question the world had asked. What was the catalyst? They may never know.

Harlow saw his face staring back as lively as it would ever be again. A dead-eyed smile on the front page of a newspaper for a report he never wanted published in the first place. She knew her face would show how shocked she was; that was fine. Let them think what they wanted about the relationship between her and Tiproil. As long as they didn't know the truth. She had gotten him killed. She had told Jane about Eden, about the secrets Tiproil had. And then, when she realized Jane would go after it, Harlow had broken into his office when no one was there to steal the key. If they had found the key, they would have left him alive, she was sure of it. He had to have known it was her who took it.

The photos published of the crime scene in the newspapers showed her final thank-you card on the floor. She saw it right away through the mess of books and papers and blood. The last day she broke into his office, she was too upset to write anything other than her name in the card. She knew he would understand; there were a million words she wanted to say, but, sometimes, it's best to say nothing at all.

As Harlow walked across the street to the car parked across from the city's new art exhibit, just out of sight from the security cameras, she reflected back for a moment on what they had accomplished. It was true; she had done a thousand things in her life that were wrong, but, now, Eden was safe, and she had finally done something good.

Harlow's only wish was Tiproil could've been around to see it, his dumbstruck face laughing back at her over a shared bottle of whiskey in his office that always smelled of tangerines and ink.

Bibliography

Curry, Andrew. "Gobekli Tepe: The World's First Temple?" Smithsonian.com. Smithsonian Institution, November 1, 2008. https://www.smithsonianmag.com/history/gobekli-tepe-the-worlds-first-temple-83613665/.

Farber, Zev. "The Cherubim: Their Role on the Ark in the Holy of Holies." TheTorah.com. https://www.thetorah.com/article/the-cherubim-their-role-on-the-ark-in-the-holy-of-holies.

Mark, Joshua J. "Uruk." Ancient History Encyclopedia. Ancient History Encyclopedia, December 31, 2020. https://www.ancient.eu/uruk/.

Mark, Joshua J. "Uruk." Ancient History Encyclopedia. Ancient History Encyclopedia, December 31, 2020. https://www.ancient.eu/uruk/.

The Human Dawn: Time-Frame. Alexandria, VA: Time-Life Books, 1991.

Lovejoy, Bess. "7 Of the World's Most Fascinating and Beautiful Catacombs." Mental Floss, December 4, 2015. https://www.mentalfloss.com/article/64564/7-worlds-most-fascinating-and-beautiful-catacombs.

"10 Oldest Bibles of All Time." Oldest.org, November 14, 2017. https://www.oldest.org/religion/bibles/

Mark, Joshua J. "Canaan." Ancient History Encyclopedia. Ancient History Encyclopedia, January 2, 2021. https://www.ancient.eu/canaan/

"How Were the Books of the Bible Chosen?" Biblica, May 12, 2020. https://www.biblica.com/resources/bible-faqs/how-were-the-books-of-the-bible-chosen/

Williams, John. "Isidore, Orosius and the Beatus Map." *Imago Mundi* 49, no. 1 (August 1, 1997): 7–32. https://doi.org/10.1080/03085699708592856

Charles, R. H. *The Apocrypha and Pseudepigrapha of the Old Testament in English: with Introductions and Critical and Explanatory Notes to the Several Books*. Berkeley, CA: Apocryphile Press, 2004

Harlitz-Kern, Erika. "9 Things You Should Know about the Oldest Bible in the World." BOOK RIOT, November 11, 2017. https://bookriot.com/9-things-know-oldest-bible-world/

Vanderkam, James, and Speer Morgan. "The Dead Sea Scrolls: The Book of Jubilees." The Missouri Review, December 1, 1992. https://www.missourireview.com/article/the-dead-sea-scrolls-the-book-of-jubilees/

"When Was the Bible Written?" Biblica: The International Bible Society, May 12, 2020. https://www.biblica.com/resources/bible-faqs/when-was-the-bible-written/

Flores, Lourdes. "Baptistery Dedicated to St. John the Baptist." Baptistery Dedicated to St. John the

Baptist. Visit Florence.
https://www.visitflorence.com/florence-churches/baptistery.html

Harris, Beth, and Steven Zucker. "The Mausoleum of Galla Placidia, Ravenna." Smarthistory. Khan Academy, March 13, 2013.
https://www.khanacademy.org/humanities/medieval-world/early-christian-art/early-christian-architecture/v/the-mausoleum-of-galla-placidia-ravenna.

"Mausoleum of Galla Placidia." Ravenna Tourism. Accessed January 3, 2021.
http://www.turismo.ra.it/eng/Discover-the-area/Art-and-culture/Unesco-world-heritage/Mausoleum-of-Galla-Placidia.

NLT: Illustrated Study Bible: New Living Translation. Carol Stream, IL: Tyndale House Publishing, Inc., 2015.

CPSIA information can be obtained
at www.ICGtesting.com
Printed in the USA
LVHW052148290321
682893LV00022B/1667